"Thank you, Mac. For the dance, for tonight, for everything," Ashley said breathlessly

He reached up and gripped her elbow, his fingers warm and strong. The consistent possessiveness of his touch thrilled her. No man had ever made her feel the way he did.

"You're welcome, Ash. And you were right. It wasn't so bad."

"See, I told you—"

He leaned close to cut her off. "Mostly because I had the chance to hold you in my arms."

Before she could decide if he was simply being complimentary out of politeness or if the shadows darkening his topaz gaze held something more, something closer to what she was feeling, she had to step ahead of him to avoid the waiters scrambling to clear the dozens of large round tables. But she had no doubt there was something between them.

Something very real, very compelling...and very *dangerous*.

Dear Reader,

It's hot outside. So why not slip into something more comfortable, like a delicious Harlequin American Romance novel? This month's selections are guaranteed to take your mind off the weather and put it to something much more interesting.

We start things off with Debbi Rawlins's *By the Sheikh's Command*, the final installment of the very popular BRIDES OF THE DESERT ROSE series. Our bachelor prince finally meets his match in a virginal beauty who turns the tables on him in a most delightful way. Rising star Kara Lennox begins a new family-connected miniseries, HOW TO MARRY A HARDISON, and these sexy Texas bachelors will make your toes tingle. You'll meet the first Hardison brother in *Vixen in Disguise*—a story with a surprising twist.

The talented Debra Webb makes a return engagement to Harlequin American Romance this month with *The Marriage Prescription*, a very emotional story involving characters you've met in her incredibly popular COLBY AGENCY series from Harlequin Intrigue. Also back this month is Leah Vale with *The Rich Girl Goes Wild*, a not-to-be-missed billionaire-in-disguise story.

Here's hoping you enjoy all we have to offer this month at Harlequin American Romance. And be sure to stop by next month when Cathy Gillen Thacker launches her brand-new family saga, THE DEVERAUX LEGACY.

Best,

Melissa Jeglinski
Associate Senior Editor
Harlequin American Romance

THE RICH GIRL GOES WILD
Leah Vale

TORONTO • NEW YORK • LONDON
AMSTERDAM • PARIS • SYDNEY • HAMBURG
STOCKHOLM • ATHENS • TOKYO • MILAN • MADRID
PRAGUE • WARSAW • BUDAPEST • AUCKLAND

If you purchased this book without a cover you should be aware that this book is stolen property. It was reported as "unsold and destroyed" to the publisher, and neither the author nor the publisher has received any payment for this "stripped book."

For my mom, because she listened to each and every one of my stories, or at least did a darn good job pretending.

ISBN 0-373-16936-1

THE RICH GIRL GOES WILD

Copyright © 2002 by Leah Vroman.

All rights reserved. Except for use in any review, the reproduction or utilization of this work in whole or in part in any form by any electronic, mechanical or other means, now known or hereafter invented, including xerography, photocopying and recording, or in any information storage or retrieval system, is forbidden without the written permission of the publisher, Harlequin Enterprises Limited, 225 Duncan Mill Road, Don Mills, Ontario, Canada M3B 3K9.

All characters in this book have no existence outside the imagination of the author and have no relation whatsoever to anyone bearing the same name or names. They are not even distantly inspired by any individual known or unknown to the author, and all incidents are pure invention.

This edition published by arrangement with Harlequin Books S.A.

® and TM are trademarks of the publisher. Trademarks indicated with ® are registered in the United States Patent and Trademark Office, the Canadian Trade Marks Office and in other countries.

Visit us at www.eHarlequin.com

Printed in U.S.A.

ABOUT THE AUTHOR

Having never met an unhappy ending she couldn't mentally "fix," Leah Vale believes writing romance novels is the perfect job for her. A Pacific Northwest native with a B.A. in communications from the University of Washington, she lives in Portland, Oregon, with her wonderful husband, two adorable sons and a golden retriever. She is an avid skier, scuba diver and "do-over" golfer. While having the chance to share her "happy endings from scratch" with the world is a dream come true, dinner generally has come premade from the store. Leah would love to hear from her readers, and can be reached at P.O. Box 91337, Portland, OR 97291, or at http://www.leahvale.com.

Books by Leah Vale

HARLEQUIN AMERICAN ROMANCE
924—THE RICH MAN'S BABY
936—THE RICH GIRL GOES WILD

Don't miss any of our special offers. Write to us at the following address for information on our newest releases.

Harlequin Reader Service
U.S.: 3010 Walden Ave., P.O. Box 1325, Buffalo, NY 14269
Canadian: P.O. Box 609, Fort Erie, Ont. L2A 5X3

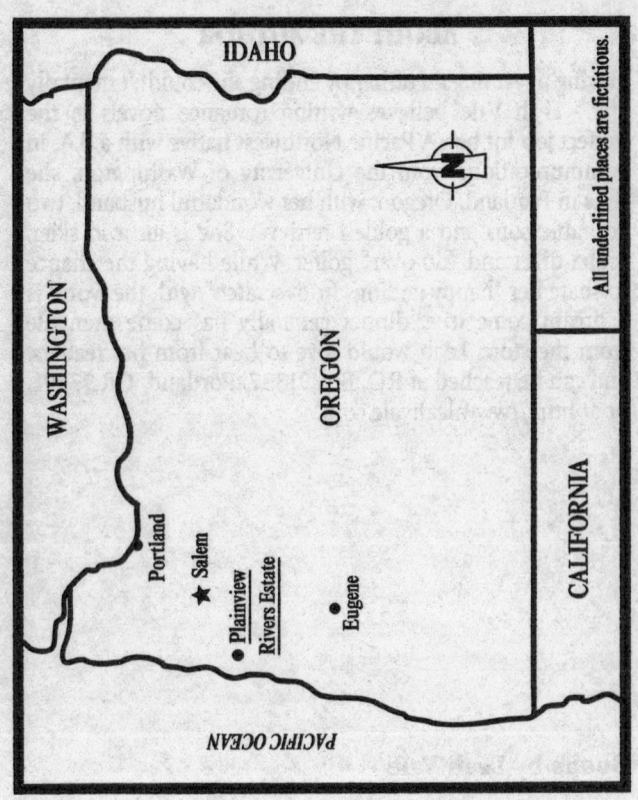

Chapter One

Bike shorts are padded, right?

The inane question was the only coherent thought Ashley Rivers could form, as she stood frozen in her descent of the grand, freestanding staircase in her family's mansion.

Granted, the fact that a strange man in full bicycling gear with a bright yellow mountain bike hoisted on his shoulder had strolled through the front door first thing in the morning, without so much as a knock or call of hello, was shocking enough. But for that man's skin-tight biking shorts and mud-caked short-sleeved Lycra shirt to hug his big, muscular body the way it did...well, it was little wonder Ashley found herself growing warm in her cream Chanel suit and incapable of thought. She practically gaped as he angled his body, well-defined muscles bunching and stretching, to close one of the oversize, dark oak, front doors behind him.

Having always preferred polish and sophistication, not to mention proper manners, Ashley should have been repulsed. She wasn't.

Far from it.

The mud splatters and dark whisker stubble on his square jaw enhanced his rugged, chiseled features the way the best makeup enhanced a woman's looks, and had, no doubt, been much easier to acquire.

He glanced up, his gaze as startling and disconcerting as his unexpected entrance and attire. His hazel eyes were the exact golden-brown of the sun-lightened streaks in his dark-brown hair hanging beneath his bicycle helmet to his collar.

Then he smiled at her.

Ashley almost dropped her day planner. His even, white teeth, and a broad grin that created deep grooves in his cheeks and a warmth in his eyes gave his looks the impact of a backboard shattering slam-dunk. The light in his gaze increased to an unmistakable, sizzling heat when he looked her over from head to foot with obvious deliberation, pausing significantly on her breasts and legs.

"Well, good morning, gorgeous." His deep voice rumbled its way up to her and made her heart do something it had never done before in her entire thirty years—skip a beat.

"Good—" Her voice sounded horribly strangled. She cleared her throat and started again. "Good morning." The ridiculous tenor of her voice was enough to shake her out of her hormonally induced stupor.

Her brain working again, she flipped open her day planner with practiced efficiency and scanned the day's schedule. Nothing about her receiving anything via messenger. Besides, what sort of messenger let himself into the house?

Belatedly realizing she should be concerned, she

leaned toward the rail and checked to see if Donavon, their houseman, was anywhere in sight. And while it was barely past seven in the morning, surely someone else, perhaps her grandmother, or her only sibling, Harrison, and his wife and son, should be up and about.

An early riser, her father would normally be in his den right off the large foyer, occupying himself with the management of the Rivers family's huge portfolio, since he'd turned over the running of Two Rivers Industries to her older brother six months ago. But Dad was out of town, playing host to a charity golf tournament she herself had put together, and wouldn't be home until next weekend.

Ashley returned her attention to the man eyeing her with far too much undisguised interest. Used to more subtle appreciation, she grew uncomfortable. The last man to so blatantly admire her, Roger Benton, had actually been calculating her net worth when they first met at a charity wine auction. She was, after all, the unattached daughter of one of the wealthiest men in Oregon. The ache of a heart that had been slow to realize Roger's true focus was a potent reminder to steer clear of such men.

She allowed herself the indulgence of the slightest frown. Crude gold digger or not, it would be impolite to scowl. Determined to be the mannerly, devoted daughter her father had once assumed her incapable of being, Ashley strove to never be impolite. "May I help you?"

The man glanced at his bike, then shrugged it off

his shoulder. "Nah. Got it handled. This bike's my baby."

His *baby's* knobby, rubber wheels bounced when they hit the foyer's once pristine black and white marble tiles and sent mud splattering as far as the round, carved marble table with its large flower arrangement in the center of the foyer. The pale yellow day lilies that made up the bulk of the arrangement bobbed as they were soundly decorated.

She pursed her lips and pulled her pen from its sleeve in the day planner. In the 8:00 to 8:15 a.m. space she wrote:

Reorder foyer floral arrangement.

She looked up in time to see him prop his filthy bike against the mahogany wainscoting. Her frown deepened despite herself. Her father loved this house, having been built by his own father to provide a home for all the members of the Rivers family, present and future. While her father accepted his grandson's wear and tear on it with surprising good humor, he wouldn't appreciate her allowing a stranger to mar so much as an inch of the place.

Before she could suggest that his bike was better suited to waiting outside on the circular driveway, the man said, "I could use some breakfast, though. Nothing like an early-morning off-road 20k—not counting the trek back up the gully I slipped down, of course—to get a guy's appetite up." He gave her another all-too-thorough look. "Though there are some things I'm always hungry for."

Ashley blinked. Surely he couldn't be implying—

An unaccustomed heat blossomed in her cheeks.

She pulled in her chin. She never blushed. *Never.* Even when she'd found her almost-fiancé, the man she'd loved, in bed with another woman and overheard his plans to use her for her money she hadn't blushed. Shook with so much anger and humiliation she'd barely been able to get the words out to end their relationship, yes, but she hadn't blushed. Now, especially, she always made sure she was far too well prepared to be so affected.

The fact that this unscheduled visitor could have such an effect on her set her in motion.

Clutching her open day planner to her chest like the shield it was, she came the rest of the way down the stairs, rounded the foyer table and firmly asked, "May I ask who, exactly, you are? I don't believe we've had the pleasure of meeting before." Though she strove to keep her tone polite, she was certain he'd catch the censure.

After all, he had simply walked into her family's home and appeared to be making himself comfortable. While making her *uncomfortable.* She would have been notified if any early-morning, 20k-minded visitors were expected. And who in their right mind would enter someone else's home in such a muddy state?

If he didn't have an excellent explanation for his presence he was about to find himself out the door and glad for his padding.

He stepped toward her, his expression definitely hungry, his sensuous lips curled salaciously.

Ashley violently wished she'd stayed on the stairs. While he had looked big from above, he was enormous on the same level. Without heels, she was considered on the tall side at five feet nine inches, but even with the sling-back, two-inch heels she was wearing this morning she had to crane her neck back to look him in the face.

She also had to marshal all of her old-world girls' school etiquette training not to fidget under the intense appreciation in his gaze, reminding herself of the unmalleable Three P's—*Propriety, Presentation, and Principle*—that had turned her into a woman her father could be proud of, one he would love. Normally the reminder helped, but even Roger had never looked at her with as much heat during their eight months together, and her own temperature rose with alarming velocity.

While she always took care to look her best so no one would doubt her capabilities, she had a hard time believing she looked *that* good. So there was no reason for her to be so...so...affected by this man's attention.

A corner of his mouth curled upward and she felt an answering tightening in her stomach. "Oh, if we'd met, sunshine, there definitely would have been pleasure, and you'd remember it."

His deep, rich and extremely provocative tone, not to mention his words, were like a warm, moist finger traveling up her spine, and it was all she could do not to shudder in the oddest sort of pleasure.

She took a hasty, and regrettably obvious, step back and pretended to consult her schedule while she struggled to gather her normally reliable wits about her. This man had the unique ability to unsettle her as easily as his filthy bike had muddied the foyer. Because her role in life had been to keep everything *settled* since her mother's death nearly three years ago, she needed to regain her control and send the fellow on his way. But first, in the 7:45 to 8:00 a.m. block she wrote:

Consult with Donavon regarding household security.

Slipping the pen back where it belonged and closing the day planner with a snap, she said, "Yes, well..." She cleared her throat, straightened her shoulders and offered him her hand. "I'm Ashley Rivers. And you are...?"

"Charmed." He enveloped her hand in his big, warm grasp and gently, with unbelievable sensuality, squeezed. "And enthralled." One of his rather wicked looking dark brows arched slightly beneath the shadow of his bike helmet. "Maybe even a little smitten. But I am most definitely—" he regained the step she'd placed between them and leaned toward her "—starved."

For the barest of seconds Ashley thought he might kiss her. The warm, minty scent of his breath unaccountably overrode the impact of his mud smell, and instead of skipping a beat, this time her heart raced in expectation—something else it *never* did.

He didn't kiss her, though. He pulled back, released her hand and asked, "Where's the kitchen?" before strolling off toward the long hall that paralleled the large foyer and led to the back of the house, his molded-sole biking shoes making an unusual *clack* on the marble floor.

Her hand trembling ever so slightly despite her best effort, Ashley reopened her day planner to the day's date, took out her pen and in the 7:15 to 7:45 a.m. block wrote:

Take extended cold shower.

MAC BEAT AS HASTY a retreat as he dared from the unexpected and potentially disastrous complication to his plan.

Damn it. How could he have forgotten Harrison had a sister? Because while he'd heard her name, he'd never met her, that's how. No man with a pulse could forget meeting Ashley Rivers.

Holy haggis, the woman was Grace Kelly, part two. Polished and poised on the outside, with her golden-blond hair pulled into a perfect bun, her flawless, even features accented with just the right amount of makeup and her jewelry obviously expensive but not overdone.

Yet the spark in the blue-green depths of her beautiful eyes...he knew in his gut after being in her presence all of five minutes that on the inside she was as strong as steel and just as fiery when heated. The sensual possibilities made him hot.

But she would rat him out in a heartbeat.

She was a creature of her world. A creature he knew all too well. He shook his head in disgust, the bitterness he'd been nursing these past weeks bubbling. He'd learned his lesson.

Following his nose to the kitchen, Mac lengthened his stride when he heard the *click-click* of Ashley's heels as she came after him. No way would a woman like her let him get away with an entrance—and exit—like that, not without pressing for details.

Right now he couldn't supply any. Her looks had thrown him for a loop when he'd come through the door, and instead of doing the simple thing by supplying her with a random name, all he could think to do was come on to her. A natural enough reaction, he supposed, considering how her tailored cream suit coat accentuated the fullness of her breasts and her slim waist. The matching, above-the-knee length skirt drew the eye to her curvy, long legs right down to her cream, sling-back pumps. Man, what a view he'd had while she'd been up on the stairs.

Judging by her pink-cheeked, wide-eyed reaction to his mild flirting, Miss Ashley might be in need of a little excitement in her life. He certainly was never averse to excitement. Had sworn to make it his goal in life, he thought grimly. Though the fact that making her blush had made him feel like he had scored a goal in a World Cup soccer match wasn't so bad, either.

Coming up with any old name but his own and a decent reason for invading the Rivers estate would have been smarter, but a more appealing idea formed in his sleep-deprived brain. Keeping Harrison's obviously repressed society sister flustered would be an excellent way to keep her from figuring out who he was.

While the confining upper-class social circles he was obliged to inhabit were on the opposite coast, based on what Harrison had said about his younger sister's big-time charity pursuits, Mac didn't doubt for a second that Ashley Rivers knew the name Wilder

Huntington MacDougal V. And why he should be in New York suffering under the glare of scandal instead of hiding out on the outskirts of quaint little Plainview, Oregon.

He'd had a hell of a time slipping away from the tabloid press, and the last thing he wanted was some society-page sweetheart dropping a dime on him.

"Excuse me, er, sir," Ashley called in such a commanding yet exceedingly polite tone he stopped his trek down the never-ending, sun-washed hall lined with French doors on one side and noteworthy works of art on the other. He turned slowly so he could control his urge to tell her to go away.

He couldn't believe she was still being so polite. By now, any of the MacDougal women would have called him a colorful name, tackled him and sat on his head until he came clean about who he was and why he was there.

The flustered look on Ashley's beautiful face as she screeched to a halt out of his reach almost made him take pity on her. Almost.

"I'm sorry, but I'm going to have to insist that you tell me who you are and what business you have here in my home, at this hour, and in that—" she waved her thick, black leather, antiquated day planner at his grubby riding gear "—that...state."

Realizing he still wore his bicycle helmet, he slowly peeled it from his head and shook out the hair he hadn't taken the time to have cut before he'd bailed out of New York. He needed to come up with a story to get her off his back, but he was distracted by how tightly she'd pulled her gorgeous golden hair into its bun at the base of her slender, elegant neck.

He stepped toward her. The urge to free her hair seized him. Which was ridiculous. Delectable women were as common as Blue Chip stocks and bonds in and around the MacDougal clan. And he'd never before felt the need to start a campaign to free repressed hair. Nonetheless, his fingers itched.

He leaned closer, catching a whiff of her delicate scent, a designer fragrance he recognized but couldn't name. Admiring her willingness to stand her ground even though he deliberately crowded her, he said, "Do you like omelets? I make a killer omelet. Let me make you a great big, fluffy one and we can get to know each other the only way a man and woman should. Early in the morning, the spring sun shining through the windows after a long night…"

She blushed vividly.

Gooooaaaal!

But since he *had* had a long night—flying the redeye, waiting forever to pick up his mountain bike and other stuff from the oversize baggage check, loading the rented SUV to the gills and arriving at his college buddy's house so early he'd decided to go for a ride through the woods surrounding the estate rather than disturb anyone—he was too beat to think of anything else to say. And she looked as if she was about to scream for the police. Politely, of course.

Cursing his idiocy for not having come up with some sort of plan beyond hiding out at Harrison's until after Stephanie's manipulative lies became apparent and their families stopped planning a shotgun wedding, he stuck out his hand and said on a sigh, "My friends call me Mac."

A freshly dried dirt clod lost its grip on his arm hairs and dropped with an ominous *thunk* between them.

She eyed his dirty hand, her posture stiff as a board, but her genetically engineered, flawless manners had her reaching for his hand. He engulfed her fair, slender and delicate hand in his big, dirty paw.

Just when their skin touched and the electricity he'd felt when she'd introduced herself earlier sparked and sent heat straight to his lap, he was hailed from behind.

"Wild Man! You're here," Harrison exclaimed.

Thank the god of good bagpipes. At last, a man whose brain might actually function around Miss Ashley Rivers.

HER HEART THUNDERED the way it had the last time this Mac person had taken her hand in his, and Ashley jumped at her brother's greeting. She tried to end the handshake that wasn't really a handshake, more a handholding, but Mac, or Wild Man, or whoever he was, wouldn't let go. When he turned toward her brother, she sent Harrison a pointed look.

Harrison raised a golden brow, took in her trapped hand, then grinned at the other man. "I see you've met my sister. The hostess with the mostest."

Not sharing her brother's sense of humor, she said, "Actually, I haven't been able to get him to tell me who he—"

Her captor turned his attention back to her and pumped her hand vigorously, a strangely relieved look shining in his hazel eyes. "The name's Mac Wild. Trust me, the pleasure is all mine."

Ashley had never heard a more fitting moniker in her life, especially compared to her brother's polished, though just as big and handsome, looks. She couldn't imagine Mr. Wild having any other name, with his unruly hair, his full-tilt enjoyment of life obvious in his muscular body, his animal magnetism that gave him such a sensuous presence...

Blinking, she forced herself to focus.

She racked her brain, but the name didn't ring a bell. And she never forgot a name. His face did look vaguely familiar, but with his model good looks, she was probably thinking of some guy in a sports drink ad.

Giving a sudden, yet no less subtle tug, she extracted her hand from his and avoided his reflexive grab. Grateful her hand came away free of mud, she asked, "How do you know my brother, Mr. Wild?"

"Call me Mac."

Harrison answered her question as he slung an arm around Mac's shoulders. "Harvard."

Ashley struggled to hide her surprise. Mac Wild looked more like a graduate of the X-Games than her older brother's alma mater.

Mr. Wild cleared his throat. "Yes, well, it's surprising what they'll let on campus." He raised an elbow and gave Harrison a rather rough-looking jostle.

Her brother let out a grunt then exclaimed, "Oh, that's right. Yes, it is."

Knowing her brother's nonjudgmental nature would lead him to befriend a janitor as easily as a fellow summa cum laude—or fall in love with and marry a wonderful girl with a very different background than theirs—Ashley refrained from inquiring about his friend's field of study.

Another dirt clod dropped from Mr. Wild's person and made Harrison retract his arm and check the underside of his no longer entirely white dress shirtsleeve.

Ashley struggled to contain a baleful sigh. "What brings you to the estate this morning?"

"Other than omelets with a pretty girl? Well, let me see…" His words trailed off as he glanced at Harrison.

Harrison gave a slight nod. "Mac's going to help me with the Dover Creek Mill modernization."

"Really," Ashley murmured as she opened her day planner, surprised at herself for having missed one of Harrison's business contacts. Her father counted on her to be on top of such things. Heaven forbid Mac had been around six months ago when she'd coordinated Harrison and Juliet's wedding. She'd be mortified to have failed to invite him, because clearly he and her brother were on good terms. And as he had intimated earlier, she would have remembered if she'd seen him at the ceremony, whether she'd met him or not. Mac Wild was not a man easily forgotten.

Harrison regained her attention by slapping Mac on the shoulder, dislodging more filth. "That's right. Mac, here, or better known as Wild Man at Harvard, is my—" he gave his friend a head-to-toe look "—my Environmental Specialist. As a favor to me, he's going to do an impact study of the changes I want to make at the mill."

Ashley nodded, not surprised that Mac Wild would make a career out of something involving dirt. The man clearly was not averse to the stuff. His choice of transportation to what undoubtedly was an arranged, early-morning, casual meeting with Harrison before her brother left for his trip made sense for an earth-conscious guy. As far as Mr. Wild's taking free rein with the Rivers's home and hearth... Perhaps he felt his friendship with Harrison gave him greater privileges.

She heaved a sigh of relief. Not only was his presence explained, but her contact with the man would be minimal. Thank goodness. The last thing she needed right in the middle of planning Harrison's two-year-old son Nathan's christening was Mac Wild's disturbing come-ons. Her hands were blessedly full as it was keeping her family's traditions thriving and everyone from floundering beneath their social and philanthropic obligations, as her mother had done before she lost her battle with cancer.

Her gaze involuntarily flicked past the front of Mac's bike shorts and her suit became too warm once again for the mid-May morning. Yes, it was a good thing she wouldn't be subjected to Mr. Wild's presence often. She didn't have the time nor inclination for distraction.

After living her entire life in Harrison's towering shadow, she wasn't about to jeopardize her father's notice and approval by losing her focus now.

And a man, especially one who could very well be cut from the same cloth as Roger, wasn't worth the risk.

Or the heartache. Discovering Roger had been using her had rocked her to her soul. She would never, ever, open herself up to that kind of hurt again.

"Oh, hey, Ash." Harrison drew her gaze. "I know you'll want to kill me for springing this on you—" To his friend he gave a conspiratorial aside, "She runs a tight ship, and likes to do that whole gift-basket, arrange-for-all-your-needs-in-advance type of thing."

Mac gave a sage nod in response, an oddly knowing look in his hazel eyes as his gaze traveled over her.

A sense of doom gripped Ashley.

To her, Harrison said, "But ol' Wild Man is going to be our houseguest for oh…" He raised questioning brows at Mac.

Mac's gaze fastened on hers, a predatory gleam making his eyes glow to a deep topaz. He neatly supplied, "No less than a month."

Ashley dug her nails into the pliable leather of her day planner but forced her expression to remain pleasant. She silently chanted the Three P's again.

Propriety, Presentation, and Principle.

"That's right," Harrison concurred. "No less than a month. Since he's doing this study as a favor to me, and all, he'll be staying here with us."

Mac reached out and pried one of Ashley's hands off her day planner, sending her body temperature through the roof. "And it'll be enjoyable, I'm sure," he practically purred before bringing her knuckles to his wonderfully sensual lips for a soft-as-you-please kiss.

For the first time in her highly refined adult life, Ashley wondered just how cold the McKenzie River, running smooth and deep at the edge of the house's vast lawn, was this time of year. And if it would be cold enough to help her resist the temptation of Mac Wild.

Chapter Two

Mac watched Ashley's perfectly bowed, lightly glossed and achingly kissable lips pucker ever so slightly before she made a visible effort to shift her features into a pleased expression. If he hadn't been staring at her mouth he would have missed it. He pulled a sardonic grin.

Then he realized that for the exceedingly proper Miss Ashley to show even that much displeasure meant she must be heaving with it on the inside. Now, he knew he wasn't *that* distasteful. Mud washed off, for saints' sake.

She pulled herself up and flashed him a brilliant smile that he suspected would have knocked him to his knees if it had been a little warmer around the edges and had reached her deep-lake blue eyes. "I'm sorry I didn't know in advance about your arrival. You would have received a much warmer—er—hospitable reception."

He smirked. Things certainly didn't need to get any warmer between them. "No worries, sunshine. The less pretenses, the better, as far as I'm concerned."

The pretenses of dating had landed him in this nightmare in the first place.

His mood sobering, he turned to Harrison. "Do you have a minute, or are you on your way to the office? I know you're the big boss, now, but you do still work Fridays, right?" They needed to get their story down so no other surprises threatened this so-far perfect escape from Stephanie and her attempt to use outright lies and scandal to land herself a MacDougal.

Harrison put a hand on Mac's shoulder. "Boy, you must be tired. I'm not going in to work today. Remember I told you that Juliet, Nathan and I are heading down to the amusement parks in southern California for two weeks? I couldn't wait any longer to take my little man to Disneyland."

Mac ran a hand down his cheek, wiping off dirt stuck to his whiskers. "That's right." He *was* tired. Had been since he'd discovered his family intended to use the situation with Stephanie to force him to settle down.

He couldn't. His heart was seared with the oath he'd made on the worst day of his life, and he wasn't about to break it for the likes of Stephanie Thorton-Stuart. Even though Harrison was leaving, Mac had come anyway because he wasn't here for a social visit. He was here to hide.

Thankfully not noticing Mac's seriousness, Harrison chuckled. "I think Juliet is about as excited as Nathan. She's never been there before, so she's vowed to hit every attraction in the place. Nathan will probably sleep through half of it."

A surprisingly soul-wrenching envy that his friend's

true love was alive and kicking broadsided Mac. Only practice kept him from doubling over with the ache. His throat constricting, he asked, "Nathan's...two now?"

Still oblivious, Harrison grinned and his chest swelled up, definitely the proud pop. "Two and cute as all get out. We don't have to leave until later this morning, so you'll get to meet Nat and his gorgeous mama. Assuming, of course, they ever get their act together and come down here for breakfast."

Ashley, who had been watching the conversation with a look that left no doubt that the wheels were noisily turning within her beautiful and clearly not so empty head, offered, "Why don't I go up and inform Juliet about your guest while you take Mr. Wild to the kitchen. He claims to be in dire need of sustenance."

Pushing away the pain he'd lived with for over a decade, Mac regrouped and returned her volley. "I'm in dire need of a lot of things, sunshine."

She smiled, but it was still tight around the edges. "Harrison will take care of you, I'm sure."

He wanted to say that there was no way in hell Harrison could take care of what she put him in mind of, but she turned crisply and headed back toward the front of the house. Mac settled for a soft whistle through his teeth and murmured, "Holy haggis."

Harrison laughed and pulled him by the arm in the opposite direction, saying in a soft voice, "Come on, Mac. Better men than you have tried to get a rise out of that one."

Unable to take his eyes off the sexy sway of Ashley's retreating backside beneath her straight, cream skirt, Mac said, "But you know I've never been able to resist a challenge, Harrison old man, especially if I'm told it can't be done."

"Yes, but Ash is in a class by herself when it comes to single-mindedness."

Mac jerked to a stop just inside the large, French Provincial-style kitchen. Maybe Ashley was in a class of two. Stephanie was proving to be very single-minded, also. Damn her scheming heart.

Heedful of the petite, gray-haired woman in a serviceable, light gray dress busily cooking pancakes at the professional range top, he said darkly, "I'll keep that in mind."

Harrison patted the small woman on the back as he went by. "Good morning, Marie."

She turned and gave him a genuine-looking smile that lit up her olive-skinned face and dark, almond-shaped eyes. "Good morning, Mr. Rivers."

"Marie, this is a good friend of mine—" Harrison indicated to Mac "—Mac, ah, Wild. He's going to be staying here for a month or so. Don't let him charm you into making him some haggis, or any of the other bizarre stuff he has a penchant for."

Mac gave Harrison his best glare. "I do not have a penchant for haggis."

"You're always mentioning it—"

"It's a family saying."

Having never met a cook—either short-order or gourmet—he didn't like, Mac smiled at Marie, hoping his pearly whites could wipe away from her mind the image of having to prepare sheep intestines. "I'm of Scottish descent. Though my family can't seem to get it through their heads that living in America since the colonial days pretty much makes us Americans."

His charm working, the older woman beamed at him. "It's a pleasure to have you here, Mr. Wild, and I'll gladly cook you anything you wish. Just let me know far enough in advance so I can purchase ingredients if I need to."

His stomach rumbled in anticipation, but Mac assured her, "You won't have to do anything special for me, Marie. I can tell by the way this kitchen smells that I'll be more than happy with what you normally prepare."

Harrison peered over Marie's shoulder. "Don't tell me you're making Nathan pancakes again. You made them for him for dinner last night. The kid is going to turn into one."

She laughed. "That baby couldn't be anything but an angel, and today our angel is getting mouse-shaped pancakes in honor of your trip."

Mac's mouth started to water. "Ooh, if I go shower, can I have one?"

"Just wash your hands. You can have as many as you'd like."

Mac grinned at her and made for the sink. "You're my new best friend, Marie."

She giggled and dismissed him with a wave, but she dumped a ton of batter on the griddle.

Harrison said, "Just eggs are fine for me, Marie."

Mac washed and then sat down across from Harrison at the breakfast table, careful not to dislodge any dirt in Marie's clean kitchen. Being in good with the cook could make a man's life very pleasant. Double-checking to make sure she was too far away to hear, he said, "I can do Environmental Specialist."

"It seemed right up your alley."

"Come to think of it, it is. Too bad I have a billion in acquisitions and mergers to oversee or I might actually try it out."

Harrison's eyebrows went up. "So you finally broke the big 'b' barrier?"

"Yep. Last quarter." Mac realized he'd puffed out his chest like Harrison had done at the mention of his son. Deep inside, Mac would have rather been a proud papa, but without Kate, that wasn't going to happen. His business would be enough. "It's been a real bear to hold on to, though. I'd gotten heavily involved in high-tech."

"As well you should, seeing as all those neat gadgets let you do your job while on the back of your mountain bike, or hanging off a cliff..."

Or dodging paternity scandals. Harrison didn't say the words, but Mac knew he was thinking them. His friend had stepped up and taken responsibility when he'd found out he'd fathered a child. But at least he'd actually had sex with the woman.

The bitterness simmering in Mac since his family had sided with Stephanie started to boil. "It's past time for my family to accept that I have no intention of ever settling down, Harrison."

His friend gave him a level look. "Kate's been gone for a long time, Mac. She'd want you to—"

"I know exactly what she wanted me to do, and I swore I'd do it," he snapped, the wound as raw as ever. But not wanting his friendship with Harrison to suffer, he reeled himself back in and after a moment, blew out a rueful breath. "I'm sorry. It's just that this has all turned into such a mess. I never even slept with Stephanie. I took her out a few times, to make my folks happy, but it was clear from the get-go she was looking to set herself up for life in the manner in which she's become accustomed."

"Do you think she's pregnant?"

Mac snorted. "No. She wouldn't risk her figure just yet."

"Then how does she think she's going to get away with claiming she is?"

"She believes my family will be eager to force me to marry her quick to put an end to the scandal."

"She doesn't know the MacDougals very well, does she?"

"No, she doesn't. Her father has had dealings with mine over the years, so she knows our bottom line, but that's about it. Unfortunately my family *is* eager to get me to settle down, but not because of any scandal. They want me to start doing my part in increasing the Clan MacDougal."

Harrison shook his head. "There's a little more to it than that, I think."

Before Mac could refute it, Marie came toward the table and set a huge, heavenly smelling pancake, complete with two little pancakes for ears, chocolate chips for eyes, and sliced strawberries forming a smiling mouth. Too bad he didn't feel like smiling back. He did give Marie the smile and the thanks she deserved, though, as did Harrison when she served him a heaping plate of fluffy scrambled eggs.

They both dug into their breakfasts and ate in silence for a while.

Mac offered, "I apologize for dragging you into this on such short notice."

Harrison answered around a mouthful of eggs. "No sweat." He swallowed, then added, "I'm sorry I won't be around right off."

After Mac polished off his pancakes, he said, "Spending time with your son is important."

"It is. And I love it." Harrison pointed his fork at Mac. "I highly recommend it, Mac."

The dark pain started creeping back out of its hole. He'd planned to head down that road once with a girl he had met in college who had shown him how to really live life. But he'd screwed up in the worst way possible. Knowing he would never be going down that road now, Mac steered Harrison elsewhere. "Finding out you have a son must have been a real shocker."

"That, my friend, is an understatement. But I wouldn't change anything for the world."

"That's great. And I really appreciate you letting me stay here. I wouldn't have imposed, but I had to get away someplace where no one would find me. And I have to admit, the whole paternity thing put me in mind of you."

"No problem."

"I just hope my family, or the press, for that matter, doesn't find me before it's obvious that Stephanie isn't pregnant."

"Your family believes her?"

"I doubt it. But they see this as an opportunity. And that's one thing a MacDougal can never pass up."

Harrison made a noise in the back of his throat. "That's the truth, if you're any indication. Talk about the perfect predisposition for a corporate raider."

Mac shrugged. "I suppose it's the same spirit that moved my ancestors to relieve the British of all that burdensome loot on the way to resettling the clan in America."

"It was probably rightly theirs, anyhow."

"My, but you *have* turned into the romantic, haven't you?"

Harrison's eyes focused on something behind Mac, and he said on a sigh, "You have no idea."

A husky, feminine voice said, "Ashley told me we have a guest."

Mac turned and met the smiling, rich brown gaze of a very pretty woman with long, light brown hair. A towheaded little boy propped on her slim hip gave him a curious stare. Mac knew immediately who they were. Between her looks and the kid being the spitting image of his father, it was no wonder Harrison was so proud.

The ache didn't bother to creep this time. It jumped straight on his neck and tried to choke him.

Mac rose to greet them as Harrison made the introductions around the last of his scrambled eggs. "Juliet, this is Mac. Mac, this is my better half, Juliet Rivers."

She smiled, transforming herself from pretty to flat-out beautiful. "Now, I don't know what they teach at Harvard, but I've learned at community college that one plus one equals two, Harrison."

Mac liked her instantly. "And this little guy doesn't need an introduction. Hi, Nathan."

Rather than getting all shy as Mac expected him to, Nathan smiled a toothy smile and pointed at Mac's shirt. "Dirt."

Juliet laughed. "Oh, you two will get along just fine. I'm so sorry that Harrison booked our trip the same time as your visit. Usually Ashley keeps him from slipping up like this."

Mac came to his friend's defense. "It's not Harrison's fault." Unsure of what Juliet knew of his situation, Mac said tentatively, "Besides, since I'm here to help with the mill..." He drifted off when Juliet raised a curious brow.

Mac looked to Harrison, who shook his head. "Sorry, bud. She knows." To Juliet he said in a low voice, "We're saying Mac is an Environmental Specialist come to help me out at Dover Creek."

"Why all the *Mission Impossible* rigmarole?" she asked.

Mac cleared his throat. "I'd rather as few people as possible know the truth."

Her shrug said *whatever*. "As few being...?"

"Just you and Harrison."

She glanced at her husband. "Dorothy?"

Harrison looked to Mac, but he shook his head, still certain the fewer who knew, the better. Besides, it'd be that much less grief he'd have to suffer from those who might think his family was right.

Harrison sighed. "As far as I can remember, Grandmother has never met Mac, and she has no reason to know who he is or why he'd be here."

Juliet's eyebrows went higher. "And Ashley?"

Mac vigorously shook his head.

Harrison concurred. "Definitely not Ashley. You know how she feels about duty to family."

Juliet smirked. "You've got a point, there." She set Nathan in a booster chair fastened to one of the seats.

The two-year-old immediately started banging on the table with his fat little hands and chanting, "Dirt, dirt, dirt."

Mac looked away.

Juliet said, "Okay, whatever you boys want to say is fine. I'll just keep my yap shut."

Mac blew out a relieved breath, wishing again that he'd thought things through a hell of a lot more. "Thanks, Juliet. I appreciate your help."

"Is there anything *I* can help with?" Ashley offered as she came through the kitchen, a ringing cell phone in her hand.

With stricken expressions, all three of them hurried to assure her there wasn't.

Ashley held the phone toward Mac. "Your bike was ringing."

"Uh, thanks." He glanced at the caller ID and fought a groan. This was his business phone and only his executive assistant, Bishop, was supposed to have the number. Damn it, had they gotten to him, also?

Knowing that simply turning the phone off as he was inclined to do would raise Ashley's suspicions, he excused himself.

By all that was tartan, he prayed that Ashley's rigid sense of propriety, the same sense that would keep her from being more than a distraction to him while he was there, had kept her from checking the display, also.

M. MACDOUG. Ashley tapped a French manicured nail against her teeth and tried to pinpoint the stirrings of recognition the name on Mr. Wild's cell phone caller ID generated. She hadn't purposefully looked at the display, but always checking her own before answering had created a habit.

Mac distracted her from her mental run through her Rolodex by heading toward the nearest door—the one leading to the wine cellar—his phone still ringing in his hand. She watched until he disappeared through the door, closing it tight behind him. She looked at Harrison and Juliet to gauge their reactions to Mac's odd behavior.

Harrison shrugged and took a swig of his coffee.

Juliet grinned and quipped, "That cellar's good for all sorts of things."

Harrison choked on his coffee. He quickly set his cup down and grabbed his wife to pull her in his lap and whisper something in her ear. Blaming the tugging sensation deep in her chest on her happiness for her brother's state of wedded bliss, Ashley rolled her eyes at their antics and went to the refrigerator to grab a muffin. Thanks to their unexpected guest, her schedule no longer held time for her usual breakfast of granola, yogurt and half a grapefruit.

Marie rounded the island toward her. "Can I get you your breakfast, now?"

Ashley waved her off. "That's all right, Marie, I'll get it."

The refrigerator door blocked her view, so she only heard Mac emerge from the cellar.

He grumbled something to the effect of, "Family,

what a pain in the—'' then broke off when he caught sight of her stepping back from the fridge to close the door.

Her curiosity running rampant, she offered, "Is there something I can be of assistance with, Mr. Wild?"

"Mac," he corrected absently as he shook his head in answer to her question. "No. It's fine. Everything's fine."

She was seized by the strangest need to show off with something she was very good at and to ease the troubled look in his golden-brown eyes. "Harrison and Juliet will vouch for my ability and willingness to handle most any situation," she pressed.

Harrison made a noise that sounded shockingly like a snort. "Better known as meddling."

Juliet came to Ashley's defense with a crude, yet effective, elbow to the ribs.

Ashley satisfied herself with the simple reminder by saying, "I don't meddle, Harrison, I *manage*." A skill that had finally earned her the only things she had ever wanted—an indispensable presence in the family business and her father's love, given in the only way he seemed capable, through his approval. And taking over after her mother's death had helped them all.

To Mac she explained, "For example, right now I'm putting together Nathan's christening ceremony and celebration. But I'm certain I could find time to help you if something has come up within the Wild family."

Harrison started to cough and choke, again. Hopefully he wasn't coming down with something before his trip.

Mac glanced from his friend to her, the corner of his mouth quirked, but he reiterated, "Really, everything is fine in the—" he coughed, too "—Wild family."

Harrison regained his breath and said to Mac, "Speaking of Nathan's christening, you should come. Since the, ah, circumstances around his birth were what they were and my name wasn't originally on the birth certificate—" he glanced at Juliet and she gave him her patent shrug "—we're having his name legally changed to Rivers and making a big deal of the christening ceremony. It would mean a lot to me to have you there."

Mac visibly blanched. "I..." He ran a hand through his long and incredibly thick hair, drawing Ashley's gaze to the unruly mass and the bunching muscles in his mud-splattered arm.

She jerked open the refrigerator's door and stepped toward the sanity-returning blast of cold air.

After a moment of heavy silence, Mac finally said, "I'm sorry, you guys, but I can't." He gave a sheepish sort of grin. "I don't have any decent clothes. I don't know about you, but I wouldn't want some bozo in Lycra or zip-off pants at my kid's shindig." He looked down at himself. "Just like I'm sure Marie doesn't want Pigpen in her kitchen. I'd better go get cleaned up."

Juliet hopped off her husband's lap and offered, "I'll find Donavon and we'll get you settled."

Mac let loose a heavy breath. "Thanks, Juliet. Harrison, if I happen to hit a bed and the bed hits back hard enough that I don't wake up until you're already gone, have a great trip. I'll catch you when you get home."

He glanced at Ashley, an unreadable expression on his face. For the first time she noticed the bruised-looking circles smudging the tanned skin beneath his eyes and the heaviness with which he moved as he followed Juliet out of the kitchen, as if all those muscles were suddenly hard to lug around.

Then he smirked at her. "Don't catch a chill, sunshine." The rough edges of his deep baritone raised the goose bumps on her skin in a way that the open refrigerator had failed to do. She started guiltily and slammed the fridge shut.

She looked at Harrison to see if he had noticed her foolish behavior, but he was watching Mac leave the room.

Harrison shifted his gaze to hers. "He was a very good friend to me in school, despite what he went through."

She raised her brows. "What did he go through?"

"He lost someone very important to him."

A pang of sympathy coursed through her heart. Surprisingly it seemed she and Mr. Wild had something in common, after all.

Before she could ask who he'd lost, Harrison added, "I'd really like to have him at my son's christening, Ash."

In other words, *make it happen.*

She would. It was what she did best.

Even though she'd prefer to keep the apparently

wounded Mac Wild as far from her family, and thus her consciousness, as possible, she gave her big brother a reassuring smile.

Thanks to her wandering gaze, at least she wouldn't be making a total guess when she gave the tailor Mac's inseam measurement.

Chapter Three

Mac rounded yet another corner in the U-shaped mansion and decided that sometimes no sleep was better than just a little. While about half the size of MacDougal House, with a pretty simple layout, the long hallways of the Rivers's home had him sufficiently lost on his way to the pool.

He shoved his long bangs away from his face, only to have them spring forward into his eyes again. He shouldn't have gone to bed for what turned out to be a five-hour nap with his hair wet, but he'd been so dog-tired that he'd barely dried off from his shower before he'd hit the sack. He usually kept his hair shorter so he never had to think about it, let alone mess with it. But barbers had been in short supply on his last scuba diving trip, and when he returned, those in Stephanie's camp had started hounding him about marrying her to the point that he hadn't wanted to take the time to have his hair cut. He'd avoided sitting still in one place long enough to give any of them an opportunity to harangue him about settling down.

Mac rolled his bare shoulders beneath the towel he'd slung around his neck, fighting the tension he'd thought he'd outrun on the cross-country flight last night. Needing more than ever to dunk his head and burn off some steam swimming laps, he lengthened his stride until his black, slip-on soccer slides slapped against his bare heels, certain he'd find the back staircase at the end of the hall that one of the maids had told him about. Supposedly it would dump him right by the door to the heated outdoor pool.

An odd tapping sound snagged his attention and he glanced into the open doorway on his right as he walked past. He jammed it into Reverse, nearly stepping out of his loosely velcroed single strap slides, until he was standing in the doorway of a room awash in muted pinks and smelling of rose potpourri. Ashley Rivers, hair still perfectly repressed and cream suit still buttoned up tight, sat at a delicate and feminine Queen Ann desk in what should have been the sitting room area of her bedroom suite.

He could see the four-poster bed, buried beneath mounds of white lace and pillows, through an open door to her right. His blood automatically started pumping in preparation. Man, this woman main-lined his libido.

She was typing away on a keyboard as she stared intently at a computer's flat-screen monitor. Sitting next to the monitor was the biggest Rolodex he'd ever seen in his life. The room even sported a file cabinet. The fact that she'd turned part of her private quarters into an office didn't surprise Mac. From the short time he'd known Ashley, he figured her the all business, no fun type.

Knowing full well Ashley Rivers was trouble and

that he should just keep on going, he instead grabbed the ends of the towel around his neck and leaned a shoulder against the doorjamb all casual-like. A perverse, hitherto unexplored aspect of his personality wanted to get back at all the Stephanies in the world, even in such a small way as, say, being an annoyance.

In his best come-here-often voice he said, "Well, hello, sunshine."

She started and glanced up. Her brow-marring expression of concentration changed into a pretty flush. He felt a jolt of satisfaction when her gaze traveled over him from head to foot and her eyes widened at the sight of him clad only in loose black swim trunks and black, foot massaging soccer slides. He indulged himself by pulling down on the towel to flex his biceps and pecs. Her flush turned into a raging blush.

Goooaaal!

Then it occurred to him that maybe she just found his epic case of bed-head offensive. Naa, it was the pecs. Clearly Miss Ashley needed to get out more.

He gestured toward the computer with an end of the towel. "What'cha doing?"

She looked back at the computer screen and blinked rapidly a few times. "I'm working," she said as if reminding herself.

"You work in your bedroom?"

"This isn't my bedroom. This is my office. My bedroom is through there." She tilted her head toward the door on her right, making her tiny, gold hoop earrings sway.

Practically salivating with the opportunities she

seemed in the habit of handing him, he grinned and rumbled, "Oh, *really*."

The way she fought to deny the suggestiveness of his tone by primly folding her hands in her lap made him decide that goading her would also be an excellent way to keep his mind off his situation and make his time here at least a little entertaining.

She cleared her throat and returned her fingers to the keyboard with a determination that made him smile genuinely.

Without looking at him she said, "Yes. And I'm quite busy, so if you'll—"

"What exactly do you do?"

She spared him a glance that said she didn't think much of his intelligence. But when that glance became a perusal of his bare chest he made sure she noticed by spreading the towel a little wider than necessary, she kind of glazed over. "I...I—"

"You...what?"

She snapped her gaze back to her desk and made a grab for her day planner. She unfastened the flap with a yank and opened it, then flipped through the pages way too fast to be able to see what was on them. "Right now I'm planning the menu for the dinner following Nathan's christening ceremony."

"Ah. And when there aren't babies to be christened...?"

"I coordinate everyone's schedules, plan social functions and put together fund-raisers for the various charities we support."

"So basically you're the Rivers family social secretary."

She straightened in her seat, visibly bristling. "I keep my family from floundering beneath their many and varied obligations, Mr. Wild. Just as my mother did."

"Mac," he insisted, his attention sliding to her Rolodex. "You must have the name and number of the entire free world in that thing." Including a MacDougal and Thorton-Stuart or two, he thought sourly.

She looked at the monstrous cylindrical file of alphabetized name cards and one side of her pretty mouth curled upward. "I do my best."

He glanced at his dive watch and decided to get her mind on something besides social connections. "Yeah, well, it's quitting time in the rest of the working world, so why don't you go pull on your swimsuit and come have a splash with me." He forced himself not to consider what that body of hers would look like in even the most modest of swimsuits.

"I have too much to do, Mr.—Mac. Which is one of the reasons my office is located where it is. For expediency's sake."

Mac was struck by how sad it was that she'd put expediency over a place to have private time in comfort. "Well, for *fun's* sake, I say you go get your suit on."

"I'm sorry, but—"

"Okay. At least say you'll go out to dinner with me later. Maybe we can even catch a movie. I'm pretty sure I saw a multiplex theater on my way through town." He surprised both of them by pressing, but her state of perpetual work was a sorry thing.

She stared at him for a moment, her eyes wide as

if he'd asked her to stuff his sporran for him while he had it on. Then she pulled her elegantly winged, blond eyebrows together the slightest bit. "Like a...date?"

He shrugged. "Whatever. Mostly we'd just be having a little fun. I promise we'll keep it casual." Casual and physical. Like the way he'd kept all his relationships since Kate.

Because a MacDougal only loved once.

It was ancient family lore, but the generations of long, successful marriages had firmly established it as fact in Mac's mind. The ache he still felt for the woman he'd committed his heart to provided further proof of the truth of the saying.

She shook her head with center-court-ref firmness. "I'm sorry, Mac, but to me, there is no such thing as a casual relationship. People deserve more from those in their lives. I believe that if you can't commit—" her voice hitched slightly and she shifted her gaze to her day planner "—the most of yourself, then you shouldn't enter into a relationship in the first place."

She ran a manicured fingernail down a page in the planner. "And right now, I don't have the time—" she looked up, this time meeting his gaze, her blue-green eyes glowing with conviction "—nor the inclination to enter into any new relationships." She rose smoothly from her embroidered upholstered chair and walked toward him, her suit looking unaccountably fresh, the gentle sway of her hips shouting confidence and emotional strength.

He figured he knew the answer, but to be safe he asked, "So you're not seeing anyone?"

"No. I'm not seeing anyone. Nor do I intend to

start. If you'll excuse me..." She grabbed the edge of her door, her finely shaped chin held high. "I have a lot of work to do."

Then she closed the door, forcing him to take a step back to keep from getting hit in the nose.

Mac stood staring at the gleaming dark wood, not used to being told no by anyone, especially a woman. Miss Ashley was going to be a tough nut to crack, but he was now more determined than ever to rise to the challenge. His pride demanded it.

He spun on his soccer slide's heel and continued on his way down the hall, telling himself it wasn't real disappointment he felt because Ashley Rivers wouldn't come out and play with him, only annoyance that she'd cut short his bid to *be* an annoyance. She clearly needed to get a life. And he was just the guy to show her what she was missing.

ASHLEY SLUMPED AGAINST the door, finally able to say what she'd wanted to say from the second she'd looked up and seen Mac standing in her doorway wearing nothing but a swimsuit and a smile. "Oh. My."

He was just too, too perfect. She pushed away from the door, peeling off her summer-weight suit jacket in an attempt to lower her temperature. No. Mac wasn't perfect, with his too long hair and too casual attitude about propriety. That wasn't what had her feeling like she'd stepped into a Swedish sauna every time he came anywhere near her.

If he wasn't perfect, what was it about him?

The image of Mac leaning against her door frame,

à la James Dean sans clothes clear in her mind, she haphazardly tossed her jacket at a white file cabinet where an overstuffed chair and ottoman had once sat. Then the answer came to her. She was simply having a base reaction to his overabundance of masculinity.

Yes, that was it, she thought as she shimmied out of her skirt, still too warm. Down to her slip, she kicked off her sling-back pumps and paced in front of her desk. While she had never been bothered before by a physical attraction—no, make that a simple *reaction*—to a handsome and, er, well-developed man, for some reason Harrison's friend had such an effect on her.

She couldn't exactly blame it on being too long in seclusion since breaking up with Roger. She had, after all, just contributed a healthy sum to one of her favorite children's charities by "purchasing" a bachelor the weekend before last. The attractive and engaging gentleman had treated her to a delightful evening in Portland that had included dinner at one of the city's finest restaurants and box seats at the opera.

Though she would have rather caught the professional basketball game that had been playing that night, she still had a pleasant enough time. At no point during the entire evening, however, had she perspired in the slightest. She had actually been quite chilled and had required her wrap.

Unfortunately Travis Norton IV hadn't affected her the way Mac did. Neither had Roger despite his intense pursuit of her and her lonely heart's response to it. No man ever had.

She put a hand to her forehead. Perhaps she was

coming down with something. Was there such a thing as studitis? She rolled her eyes at her own silliness. She simply needed to strengthen her resistance to men like Mac so she wouldn't be so affected by his magnetism during his stay at the estate.

She wasn't worried about his charm. Her heart was locked up too tight to be in any peril.

She hurried to her desk and opened her day planner. In the 6:00 p.m. space she wrote:

Rent *Indiana Jones* series and Brendan Fraser's *George of the Jungle*.

She closed her day planner with a decisive snap. If a hearty dose of handsome, unrestrained movie men didn't do the trick, then she would go back to her original plan of keeping as far away from Mac Wild as politely possible.

THE NEXT NIGHT, ASHLEY headed toward the dining room, pleased with how well her plans regarding a certain houseguest were going. She'd managed to avoid him the remainder of the night before and hadn't encountered him once today. She'd found that taking note of an odd prickling at the base of her neck allowed her to leave a room bare moments before Mac entered it. That and keeping an ear out for the odd way he tended to whistle softly through his teeth as he made his way through the halls kept her one step ahead of him and let her know which knocks on the door to her rooms to ignore.

Having spent the majority of the night before overloading on cinematic stud-muffins, she felt she was suitably immune to Mac's animal magnetism and could dine with him tonight. Thankfully her grandmother would be there as a buffer.

Stopping right before she reached the open double doors to the dining room, she smoothed the front of her pink satin, sleeveless shell and checked the fall of the matching chiffon palazzo pants. She stopped herself and let out a disgusted sigh. She did *not* care what Mac Wild thought of the way she looked, so there was no point in fussing. She didn't even know for sure if he'd be eating with them. She'd had a plate sent up to his room the night before, and he might prefer to dine that way again.

Determined to put an end to her foolishness once and for all, Ashley stepped into the doorway of the dining room muttering The Three P's. She forced herself not to pause for more than the barest of seconds at the sight of Mac. He stood facing her on the other side of the long table that ran parallel to the doors, his big, tanned hands resting casually on the back of one of the Chippendale side chairs. His hair looked as if he'd finger combed it back from his face, which added to the casual, and disturbingly appealing, style set by his white cotton shirt, the long sleeves of which he'd shoved up on his muscular forearms.

Reminding herself that she'd effectively squashed any and all physical effect he had on her, she stopped on the opposite side of the table and smiled genuinely. "Good evening, Mac."

His brows went up. Then his gaze traveled over her.

"Whoa, look at you. Going out to some charity function?"

"No. I—" *Dressed up to impress you.* She struggled not to frown at the impertinent voice in her head. She had *not* dressed to impress him. "I prefer to adhere to tradition and dress for dinner." She inwardly cringed. Her reasoning sounded lame even to her own ears, but she refused to admit that she had tried to look her best for this, this *guy*.

"Boy, did I miss that memo. Though I can't say that I'm surprised." He glanced down at himself. "I hope zip-off pants won't get me tossed out on my ear. Like I told Harrison, I kind of packed light for this trip."

She thought of the surprise she had for him and a spurt of satisfaction pushed aside the fear that she had craved his admiration. "I believe I can help you with that. But first, please, do sit down."

"Ladies first." He pulled out the chair in front of him. "The little name thingys really help a guy out when there are so many chairs."

He had indeed pulled out the chair at the place setting bearing her name placard. His sarcasm was unmistakable. What had possessed her to have Donavon lay out a formal table?

Raising her chin as if everything was as it should be, Ashley rounded the table and took her seat. She was careful not to look at Mac, keeping her focus on the fine bone china set atop a brass charger in front of her. But she could do nothing about the goose pimples that erupted on every inch of her when he bent low, his breath minty smelling and warm on her neck, to push her chair forward.

He had to be doing it on purpose. He just had to be. There was no way a man like him didn't know exactly how he affected women.

The thought gave her the bravado she needed to look over her shoulder and give him a raised brow.

Obviously getting her *step back, please* message loud and clear, he straightened away, though his smile was smug.

He made a grand show of perusing the remaining placards, which was silly since there were only two others. His had been set directly across from her, with her grandmother at her side.

He went around to his place, but eyed the one next to her. "Hmm. Well, I guess this is okay. Though I have to admit, the thought of rubbing elbows—among other things—with you does appeal. I'm a lefty, you know."

Ashley swallowed as delicately as possible, unable to pull her gaze from his. "No, I didn't, actually. But now that I do, I'll be sure to seat you at the end next time." She pointed to the distant end of the table, her smile masterfully sweet.

He raised a brow of his own, and she knew he realized she meant *far away from me*. Any retort he might have made was withheld when Donavon, in his standard white dress shirt and black slacks, came in through the butler's pantry from the kitchen carrying appetizer plates of arugula and shrimp. Thank goodness he hadn't dressed more formally. Then their guest would have reason to think she had a need to impress him.

She much preferred being in control of the situation with Mac, and smiled broadly at Donavon when he set their plates in front of them. "Donavon, since Grandmother appears to be running late—" *darn her anyway* "—would you please bring me the package that arrived this afternoon?"

"Of course," Donavon replied.

She watched the tall, slender man who'd been their houseman for as long as she could remember, yet never seemed to change, leave the room before she looked back at Mac. The expression on his face oozed suspicion. What did he have to be suspicious of?

Before she had a chance to consider the question, Donavon returned with the large, rectangle box. She'd already inspected its contents when it arrived via overnight delivery service and made sure nothing was missing or could garner complaint from its recipient.

She stood, bringing Mac out of his seat, and accepted the box from Donavon so he could get back to helping Marie in the kitchen. She rounded the table to Mac's side and set the box on his chair, her heart pounding with excitement over giving him a gift. No, she was excited about fulfilling her brother's wishes, that was all.

She avoided Mac's gaze nonetheless. "Now, before he left, my brother expressed his desire to have you attend what will be a very special event for our family, Nathan's christening. With the goal of fulfilling my brother's wishes in mind, I ordered you a suit from the tailor we use exclusively." She lifted the dark-brown, summer-weight wool suit jacket from the box and held it up to him. "Granted, it's off the rack, but it's from an excellent designer and I think the tailor was able to alter it to fit you based on my estimates of your measurements."

Mac looked from the jacket to her. "My measurements? As in my *inseam?*" He took a step forward until her knuckles were touching his hard chest as she held the jacket up for him, his topaz eyes lit with sensual mischief. "Tell me, Miss Ashley, exactly when did you take an estimate of my inseam?"

Ashley's face caught fire with the knowledge that she had indeed looked enough at his body to feel quite comfortable guessing at his measurements. She became extremely aware of the heat seeping up her arms from where her knuckles touched his chest.

She stammered, "I...you...you're similar in height and build to my brother, and having ordered clothing made for him on more than one occasion...I...well, it's just something I'm good at."

"Ah. But next time, promise me you'll take the measurements the old-fashioned way. One inch at a time."

The image of running a measuring tape up the inside of Mac's naked leg flashed vividly in Ashley's brain. She draped the jacket across his broad chest and took a desperate step back. So much for taking control of the situation.

Mac grabbed the jacket to keep it from falling to the ground, his initial annoyance at her pulling an end run to get him to go to the christening giving way to amusement. She *was* fun to fluster. And she was smart.

She'd outmaneuvered him big time. Granted, he was sure he'd be able to come up with another reason to skip out on the ceremony. Avoiding occasions that made him yearn for what might have been was something *he'd* become good at. But he still admired her cleverness.

He was beginning to like the uptight Miss Ashley.

Pushing aside the unwelcome thought, he put one arm in the jacket. "Help me on with this, will you?"

He turned his back to her and bent his knees so she could reach to guide his other arm into the jacket and pull it up onto his shoulders. He adjusted it until it settled perfectly on his frame. It fit. Not that he was surprised.

He shook his head and turned back to face her, watching her intently as she fussed with the lay of his lapels. Damn, but she was pretty. Pretty, sexy, clever. And for the strangest reason, it struck him that she was nothing like the ruthlessly ambitious Stephanie after all.

Whoa. Time to back off, Wild Man.

She glanced up and met his gaze for a second and awareness crackled between them before she dropped her attention back to his lapels. She could sure rev his engine. All he had to do was pop the clutch.

While he had every intention of keeping his foot down firm on the clutch pedal, the stupid devil inside that made him hang from cliffs without a lifeline made him lean toward her sweet-smelling hair. "I can't help but wonder what else you're good at, sunshine."

Her lush, pink lips moved, but nothing came out. He had just decided to momentarily suspend his decision to back off and put her out of her misery with a big, fat kiss when a feminine voice sounded from the doorway.

"Children, so sorry to make you wait."

Mac jerked his head up and Ashley took a hasty step back as an older woman who had to be Dorothy Rivers swept into the dining room wearing deck shoes, white Capri pants, and a nautical-looking sweatshirt. Harrison had talked a lot about his diminutive grandmother and all the activities she still engaged in, but Mac wasn't prepared for the whirlwind the Grand Dame of the Rivers clan turned out to be. And the sharpness in her dark-green eyes as she settled her gaze on him had him furthering the distance between him and her granddaughter.

Ashley recovered first. "That's all right, Grandmother. As you can see, we weren't ready to eat quite yet."

Dorothy's gaze went from Ashley to Mac knowingly. "Oh, yes, I see."

Ashley gestured to Mac. "Grandmother, this is Mac Wild. He's a friend of Harrison's. They met at Harvard. Mac, I'd like you to meet my grandmother, Dorothy Rivers."

Ever the hostess.

Dorothy extended a frail hand that revealed her age far more than her face did. "I know who this young man is." Her wink was playful, but when Mac took her hand in his, the hard squeeze she gave him made him blink and look more closely at her.

Holy haggis. She knew who he really was.

She nodded, verifying the horror undoubtedly reflected in his eyes. "I met his parents once while visiting Harrison at school. Delightful family you have, young man, but they were so concerned by your risky behavior."

"Oh?" Ashley asked with far too much interest for Mac's liking.

He started racking his brain for a place he could go and hide out instead of the Rivers estate.

Dorothy smiled and said, "That is such a handsome suit coat on you."

Surprised that she hadn't elaborated on his family for Ashley's benefit or called him Wilder, Mac answered stupidly, "Ashley bought it for me."

Dorothy clapped her hands together. "How fortuitous. I happen to have the perfect place for you to wear it."

Dread crept up his neck. "Oh?" he flatly echoed Ashley's earlier question.

Her green eyes twinkling in the dining room chandelier's light, Dorothy said, "I need Ashley to fill in for me at a dinner next Friday night—that is all right with you, isn't it, darling?"

"But you're receiving an award, Grandmother. Are you certain you can't make it?"

Dorothy waved her off. "Oh pish. You deserve that award more than I do, and something more important has come up."

Ashley hedged, "Well, if you're certa—"

"You are such a dear." Dorothy patted her granddaughter on the arm. "And Mac, you can be her escort."

Not a good idea. Spending an evening with Ashley

would not equal backing off. Mac shook his head. "I can't—"

"You know," Dorothy cut him off. "It has been too long since I spoke to your parents. How are they?"

On to her game, Mac dropped his chin and obliged. "They're fine. I'll tell them you said hello. And actually, I'd be delighted to escort Ashley Friday night." Realizing he might still have an out, he added, "Assuming, of course, that it's all right with Ashley..."

Instead of screaming foul as he'd hoped, Ashley raised her chin a notch and met his gaze, her eyes glinting with determination. "I think that would be fine, Grandmother, because I know it is customary for the recipient to have a...an escort."

Mac nearly laughed at her refusal to say *date*.

"Oh, thank you, darling. Now you two sit down to your dinner. I won't be joining you after all. Thelma Jacobson has returned from her trip to the beach and is having an impromptu clam feed, so I'm off to stuff myself on steamers. It was a pleasure to finally get to meet you, *Mac*," she ended lightly, though ominously to his ears, before she hurried back out of the dining room.

Mac rolled his shoulders beneath his new suit jacket. Great. Not only did he have to contend with Ashley, but now he was being blackmailed by a granny.

He looked to Ashley. She wore a pleasant enough expression, but he could tell she was itching to dare him to complain about ol' Dorth. He decided to make her pay, instead. The MacDougal way.

Because it seemed he'd jumped from one meddling clan to another, and damn if he wasn't attracted as hell to their fair young ringleader.

Chapter Four

"Boy, this veranda sure has a gorgeous view."

Mac's deep voice breaking the morning silence behind Ashley startled her so much she jerked. A good portion of the hazelnut-flavored coffee she'd been seeking consciousness in slopped onto her cup's saucer.

She turned in her chair, away from the view of the sprawling back lawn, to find Mac, dressed in a white, short-sleeve T-shirt tucked into black knit sweatpants above high-tech, all terrain hiking shoes, and standing just outside one of the many French doors opening on to the veranda.

He was looking directly at her, not the view.

Her system received the sort of jolt caffeine could never give her.

She pretended to misunderstand his statement. "The gardeners *have* done a stunning job with the grounds, haven't they?"

He moved toward her, plowing a hand through hair that appeared damp in the morning sun, with the comb lines still visible on the side he wasn't disrupting, like he'd just showered. His smile was lopsided and devastating. "Wouldn't know." He shrugged. "Haven't noticed."

She hid the heat his appreciation generated in her cheeks, along with the annoyance at herself and at him for affecting her so, by turning back toward the view of the lawn and taking a sip of coffee. She did make a quick check that her navy-blue skirt hadn't ridden too far up her thighs and that the pointed collar of the matching blouse hadn't opened too wide, though. No reason to let him think she was a willing participant in his pointless game. She did not need the flirtatious attention of some gorgeous *wild man* to know she had value.

When she felt certain her voice would remain steady, she offered with an encompassing wave of her hand, "Feel free to take a hike—or a stroll, if you'd prefer—around the grounds, then. They really shouldn't be missed."

He strolled right up to her instead. Releasing a noisy breath and looking out across the lawn, he leaned his sweats-clad hip against the side of her chair back and crossed his arms over his broad chest. The cedar deck chair creaked in protest. In the stillness of the morning she could easily smell his clean, slightly spicy scent and feel the heat radiating from his big body. He had indeed just showered, and she had never smelled anything so good in her life. She would have groaned if she could.

Instead she pulled in a bracing breath of crisp morning air, ignoring his smell. She focused on the faint scent of mowed grass, newly bloomed roses and the silent river flowing at the opposite end of the sloping lawn from where she sat on the raised, white veranda.

But every nerve ending she possessed tingled from his nearness. She shifted away on the cushioned patio chair and tried to regain her equilibrium by concentrating on the sun glinting off the new, shiny, dark leaves of the ancient oak tree that served as the lawn's centerpiece. Of its own volition, her gaze dropped to the base of the old tree, a favorite spot for Nathan's endless array of outside toys. She could see an oversize, orange plastic bat and a dragon pull-toy lying around the tree's massive trunk.

The yearning for a child of her own that had begun when her nephew entered their lives last summer pulsed in her womb. She yanked her gaze away. Longing for a man's touch was bad enough. She had to get a grip. Nothing but biology at work, she told herself.

And her determination to put such wants behind her was stronger. She would behave like the pleasant, mature adult she was, without letting Mac's appeal affect her.

She turned to look up at him, forcing herself to meet his gaze directly. "Did you need something?"

His mouth quirked and his topaz eyes grew hot as his gaze traveled over her, but instead of the suggestive response she'd accidentally set herself up for, he blinked lazily, looked out at the lawn and declared, "You owe me."

"Excuse me?"

He heaved a noisy breath and glanced down at her like she was a child. "I said, you owe me."

Uncomfortable with the notion of owing Mac anything, she lowered her brows. "What could I possibly owe you?"

"If I have to do something that you like, then you have to do something that I like. And while off the top of my head I can think of—" he eyed her wickedly "—a *lot* of things I'd like to do with you, today, I'd like to go mountain biking."

Certain she'd suffer a cardiac arrest if he shared even one of those other things he'd thought of, she closed her eyes, shutting out the sensuous curve of his mouth and her body's response to all the possible uses he might find for it.

She should have had Marie make the coffee double strength, because she clearly wasn't her usual self yet. She shook her head and sent her pearl drop earrings swinging. "I'm not following you."

"Oh, on a bike, you definitely will, and I imagine you won't mind the view too much, either," he quipped. Her eyes snapped open in time to see his mouth curling in a suggestive smile.

What that view would entail presented itself quite clearly in her imagination, so she adverted her eyes to erase the image and said succinctly, "I do not owe you anything, let alone a bike ride."

"Oh, yes, you do. If I'm going to escort you to that charity thing Friday—"

Her gaze leapt back to his. "That's not because of me. Grandmother is the one—"

"Why? Does she think you can't get your own date? Oh wait," he supplied before she had the chance to do more than open her mouth to protest, "I forgot, you don't date. You don't have time."

The burn of indignation had her out of her seat in a flash. Unfortunately she still had to look up to meet his mocking gaze. "I don't have time to commit to a serious relation—"

"So your grandma has to fix you up. I understand." He patted her shoulder, his hand big and warm and obnoxiously patronizing.

It took all she was worth not to kick him. "My grandmother does not have to fix me up."

"Oh, really? If your grandma hadn't appointed me to the job, who would you take, then, since you said it was customary to have an escort to this shindig?"

Her gaze trapped in his tiger-eyed stare, she stammered, "Well, I—I—"

His eyes narrowed. "Tell the truth."

She raised her chin, his challenge to her principles returning her to her senses. "I model my life around three things, Mr. Wild. The unmalleable Three P's I was taught in prep school: Propriety, Presentation and Principle. So I *always* tell the truth."

A muscle in his clean-shaven jaw flexed before he blinked slowly. "Do ya, now?" he drawled in a way that reminded her of a Scotsman. "Even if the truth is...impolite?"

She stepped away from him, using the excuse of needing to set her cup and saucer down on the small round table between two nearby chairs. "There are always ways to phrase the truth so as not to offend—"

"Who would you take?" he pressed.

She went back to her chair and picked up her day planner off the arm, using the excuse of holding it against her to cross her arms over her chest. "My father. I would have asked my father to return early from his trip to Palm Desert to escort me." She firmly added, "Since the award is honoring Grandmother, and she can't attend, it would be appropriate for my father and I to be there in her stead."

"Ah." He nodded. "Appropriate. Still, it's something you like, so fair is fair. You have to do something I like." He abruptly brought the conversation back to his original demand. "And I like to mountain bike."

"I have to do no such thing." She straightened her shoulders to counter her petulant tone. To regain her composure, she tucked her planner under her arm and retrieved her coffee cup and saucer. The near translucency of the fine bone china was a potent reminder of its worth and her role in life. "Besides," she added evenly, "I don't own a bike, let alone a *mountain* bike."

"I'm sure we can scrounge up one somewhere on this estate." He waved an unconcerned hand at the grounds.

While there were several outbuildings, including a boathouse down on the river, they were all artfully concealed by trees and hedges, and meticulously inventoried annually by her and Donavon for insurance purposes.

She shook her head as vigorously as maturity would allow. "I'm afraid not. Except for perhaps a child's bike. Some years ago I donated all of our unused sporting equipment to one of our charities. Harrison and I have simply grown—" she would have loved to say *up*, but the *pleasant* part of her plan wouldn't allow it "—too busy for such pastimes. Though we did keep our skis and our golf clubs, of course."

He made a soft, but definitely derisive noise. "Of course." He pushed off from her chair and planted his hands on his hips, pulling the fabric of his white T-shirt tight across his chest. His well-developed pecs and—heaven help her—his hardened nipples were clearly evident.

China rattled.

"So you won't square up with me because you don't have a bike."

"We have nothing to *square up*. I can't go riding with you because I don't have a bike," she corrected.

He stared at her long enough that the silence became uncomfortable. Ashley was about to break it with another apology she'd have to work at making sound genuine, but Mac dropped his hands from his hips and with surprising cheerfulness said, "Well, if you don't have a bike, I'd better get going. See ya later."

He turned and reentered the house nowhere near as quietly as he'd emerged.

Ashley pulled her chin back. She would have thought for sure that he would argue his point more, that he would have tried harder to get his way. He definitely seemed the type. He was also undoubtedly the type who would pursue her with a tenacity she'd swear was born of genuine caring, until a hopeful, foolish heart started to believe. The type who'd keep her awake all night, tossing and turning, the wicked gleam in his topaz eyes promising a damp-palmed excitement even Roger hadn't quite generated.

She took a shaky sip of her now tepid coffee. But he hadn't pursued her. Apparently he hadn't wanted to spend time with her *that* badly. The most asinine disappointment flooded her.

She clenched her jaw. She would not care whether or not Mac wanted to spend time with her, because she knew now, after spending a near sleepless night thinking about him, that spending more time than she absolutely had to with him was a bad idea.

Unfortunately she was duty-bound to help Grandmother out. She had no choice but to go with him to the banquet. That didn't mean anything need come of it, though.

MAC HEADED FOR THE STAIRS to go up to his rooms, mentally calculating how much cash he had left. He didn't want to use his bank cards unless he had no choice. He wouldn't put it beyond the press Stephanie had fired up to put a trace on them. If memory served, he had exactly three hundred and seventy-eight dollars. More than enough to stage his own end run on pretty Miss Ashley in true MacDougal fashion. He smirked in satisfaction as he took the stairs of the main staircase two at a time.

She thought she was in the driver's seat because she'd bought him a suit, eliminating his excuse for not being able to attend little Nathan's christening. Well, he'd do the same to her by eliminating her excuse for not doing what he wanted. She'd surely find another way to avoid going riding with him, though, just as he intended to avoid going to the christening. He wouldn't be pushing the issue if he believed otherwise.

There was no way they needed to spend any more time together than necessary. Ashley tempted him in ways he hadn't been tempted in a decade, ways he was better off avoiding for his plan's sake. Not to mention his oath to Kate.

He blasted into his comfortable suite of rooms, done up in very masculine, horse and hunter type darker earth tones, undoubtedly to appeal to male houseguests. All Mac cared about was that the big bed and the overstuffed armchairs in the sitting room were comfortable and that the remote to the thirty-six-inch TV worked.

Snatching his money clip and keys off the dresser, he headed back out. His pride demanded he get back on top with Miss Ashley, however. The thought brought to mind an incredibly erotic image that sent the blood that should be fueling his brain heading elsewhere. Great. He'd slip up for sure running around with a light head and heavy lap.

Too bad neither one of them could get out of Grandma Dorothy's request. Ashley's overdeveloped sense of duty would make her show, and Mac had no desire to be busted by the crafty old gal. Why she'd want him on her granddaughter's arm for a night was a mystery to him. Maybe he wasn't the only one who thought Ashley needed to get a life.

The saints help him if anyone else in attendance at the charity function knew him.

He'd just have to be charming, polite, and keep his head down as much as possible so as not to draw attention. He doubted *I never lie* Miss Ashley would let him walk away alive if she found out he wasn't being honest with her.

Why he cared was also a mystery.

LATER THAT MORNING, Mac whistled through his teeth as he came through the front door into the mansion, on a mission to haul Ashley outside to see his *gift* to her. She would have to admit, or *phrase the truth so as not to offend,* that she flat out didn't want to go mountain biking with him. Then things would certainly go easier for him when it came time to pass on the christening ceremony at the end of the month.

Mac headed straight for the main staircase, figuring he'd find Ashley toiling away in her office instead of out enjoying such a great spring day like a sane person. Like people who knew there wasn't always a tomorrow to do the things that are so often put off.

A clank followed by a distinctly feminine curse came from a room off the large foyer and stopped him in his tracks. He turned and headed for that room instead of the stairs.

Pushing aside the partially open door, he found Ashley rising up next to a massive mahogany desk set atop an intricately designed burgundy-and-cream area rug. The desk served as the main attraction in the middle of a large, well-appointed study. Two chairs upholstered in burgundy leather paid homage to the desk and its commanding, black leather chair. Larger, matching wing chairs were off to the side, facing a fireplace with an ornately carved mahogany mantel that matched the room's hardwood floor and the paneling in the foyer.

There must be a rain forest with some serious bare patches because of these people. And he'd thought MacDougal House was bad. Though his ancestors had tended more toward the marble look. Maybe they had liked the way bagpipes echoed off the stone. To Mac, the place reminded him too much of a mausoleum to want to spend any time there. At least, that's what he told everyone.

Ashley caught sight of him and froze, her hair glinting gold in the sunlight shining through the large windows filling most of one wall. Her silky, dark-blue blouse and skirt hugged her curves in the most sinfully respectable way, reminding him of the hottest pinup models from the forties. His body responded immediately like a lonely G.I.'s.

He raised a brow at her. "Did I just hear you say *oh, poop?*"

She readjusted her stance and squared her shoulders, then held up a thick-handled, silver letter opener with a lethal-looking blade. "I dropped this."

Coming into the room, he made a very obvious inspection of her sheer nylon-clad legs, starting at the hem of her knee-length skirt down to the tips of her matching, pointy-toed shoes. "I'm going to assume that if you had dropped it on your toe, you would have let loose with a little more colorful expletive."

She hefted the opener. "I'm sure I would have been in too grave of pain to say much of anything. So fortunately, I didn't drop it on my toe. But I'm afraid my father has a new dent in his floor. Wouldn't you know it would miss the rug." She toed the gleaming hardwood floor at the edge of the area rug with her pump.

Mac's mouth watered over the curved calf her pointed foot created. He buried his hands in his sweatpants pockets and moved to stand in front of the desk.

Reminding himself she had a major one-up on him, he nodded toward the opener. "You handling George's mail?"

She lowered her chin and stared at him as if waiting for him to add *like a secretary*. Clearly he didn't need to.

When he raised an eyebrow at her, she firmly set the opener on the desk. "Actually, no. I came in to update his calendar. He's been asked to play in another golf tournament, and he called from Palm Desert to have me write it down for him. In the process, I knocked the letter opener off with my sleeve." She shook out the winged cuff of her blouse.

"Sounds like you need to buy George a pocket calendar."

Her delicate blond brows twitched downward, but before she could justify her existence he added, "So you about done in here?"

She hesitated, oozing suspicion. "Yes. Why?"

"Good, because you need to come with me." He took her hand, ignoring how well it fit within his own, and started pulling her toward the door.

She resisted. "Where?"

He gave a gentle tug that got her going, the urge to stroke her palm with his thumb a bear to squelch. "Just out front. It'll only take a second."

"I'm glad, because I have a meeting scheduled with the caterer I've hired for Nathan's christening, and I don't have time for—"

"I just have something I want to give you." He opened the front door and pulled her out onto the landing. With a flourish, he extended a hand toward the fluorescent pink mountain bike parked on the drive three steps down. "Ta-da!"

Ashley stared at the bike, the tiniest of lines forming between her brows and at the edges of her mouth.

Finally she slanted him a look and asked, "What is this?"

He knew she meant his intent, but he goaded her by saying patronizingly, "It's a bicycle, Ashley."

"I know that."

She pulled her hand from his and he was dense enough to regret it.

As if to keep them safe from him, she folded her hands together in front of her and eyed him like a stern prep school principle. "What I want to know is why. What's this all about?"

"I bought it so you can go on a bike ride with me. Kinda like you buying me that nifty suit so I can go to that christening thing. And the charity thing, too. That was very...*considerate* of you, by the way."

She made a face that said *ah,* but no sound came out. She looked him in the eye for a long moment, and Mac had the uncanny impression she could see right through to his motives. A woman as gorgeous as Ashley with the ability to understand him would be a dangerous thing, indeed. Kate had been the only one to come close, and look what that had got her. He clenched his jaw and contracted his abs to contain the aching guilt.

A slow, sugary smile bloomed on Ashley's beautiful

face and Mac knew he was screwed. Why did he keep forgetting this was Harrison's sister? There wouldn't be many dumb fish swimming around in that particular gene pool.

She shifted her attention to the bike and glided down the front steps to get a closer look at it. She moved around it, running her slender, graceful hand—tipped with the most perfectly done nails he'd seen a woman sporting—from the seat to the straight handlebars. If she ever decided to run her hands over him that way...well, a big old plastic lobster bib would have come in handy right about then.

With the mountain bike between them, she met his gaze, her eyes looking dark blue thanks to her clothes and the mischief she was obviously up to. "I love it, Mac. Especially the color. This is very, very generous of you."

She was playing him, but he still felt a surge of satisfaction from being able to give her something. Which was stupid, because that wasn't why he'd done it. "It's just your basic, entry level mountain bike." He shrugged at the even stupider need to explain himself, but a woman like her expected far more expensive gifts. "I spent the morning driving around looking for a specialty bike shop—"

"I'm not sure Plainview has one."

"It doesn't. I know that now. I had to settle for buying one at that discount super-store place. Besides, it was all I could afford at the moment."

The catlike look on her face fell. "Oh, Mac, then you shouldn't have." She hurried around the bike and up the steps, her eyes big and her full lips parted in concern. "It wasn't necessary—"

His pride bristling again, he waved off her concerns and their unexpected effect on him. He was a flippin' billionaire, for saint's sake. And so what if she was decent enough to care about his financial state? As soon as the mess with Stephanie blew over he'd never see Ashley again.

He crossed his arms over his chest. "Yes, it was. I wanted to give you something, too. Now we're even. And I'll understand if you don't want to go for a ride with me. You have that meeting with the caterer, and everything."

Mac realized he'd blathered too much the second the knowing, superior look returned to her eyes, the blue-green unmistakable so close.

She tapped a manicured nail against her chin. "You know, now that I think of it, the caterer did express a desire to meet tomorrow, rather than today, but I usually prefer to get things done sooner not later. If I called and rescheduled, however, I'm sure she'd be receptive to the change."

Ashley gave a curt nod, letting him know in no uncertain terms that she'd made up her mind. "I believe I'd like to go on a bike ride with you today, Mac. Because you're right, it is only fair." She turned on her fashionably curved heel and started back inside. "I'll make my phone call, change, then meet you back down here in...say, half an hour?"

He nodded stupidly and watched her sweep back in the house.

Score another one for Miss Ashley.

He had to admire her spunk. Which was bad. He didn't want to admire anything about Ashley Rivers that wasn't a part of her anatomy. She was far too much a product of her world. A familiar world that had left him with nothing but bitterness, a world that he had every intention of keeping the hell away from.

Chapter Five

Careful not to ding-up the bikes, Mac settled Ashley's new bike on top of his in the back of the rented Explorer. With the back seat folded down, both bikes just fit on their sides. A bike rack would have been nice, but this would do.

He planted his hands on his hips as he did a quick inventory of the biking gear he'd already put in the car. With the necessary items—bikes, helmets, water bottles and repair kits—loaded, he probably had time to go ask Marie to throw together something to eat for them to take along. Despite her assurances, a woman like Ashley would need more than a half an hour to change. Appearances clearly meant a lot to her. It had taken him all of five minutes to pull on his bike gear. Who knew what sort of getup Ashley would come out in.

He blew out a derisive breath at the mental image he concocted of what Ashley would probably change into. Something pressed and pleated and impractical. Silk wouldn't surprise him. Neither would a scarf, with horse bridles and French horns on it. Something oh-so-appropriate for a woman of her bloodlines.

He looked up at the Tudor style brick mansion. While it was impressive with its multiple peaks, gray stone steps leading dramatically to large, carved doors, and many of the windows topped with genuine stained glass in the dark-red hues of the brick, the place wasn't near as ostentatious as MacDougal House with its Upper East Side address. Though it was a damn sight homier than his studio loft in SoHo, even without a Dean and DeLuca's around the corner.

His stomach automatically growled at the thought of the gourmet grocer. Despite easy access to great food, his apartment held little appeal other than a convenient staging ground for his gear and a place to just be. SoHo wouldn't have been his choice, but it had been Kate's. So he'd hung on to the place she'd made a deposit on but never had a chance to move in to.

His appetite immediately gone, replaced by a familiar emptiness he could never fill, Mac forced his attention back to the modest—relatively speaking—mansion in front of him. He decided the Rivers's home couldn't be more than fifty years old. New money. Maybe Ashley's bloodlines weren't so noteworthy. Mac shrugged and turned back to the Explorer. All he'd cared about when he'd met Harrison was that he had a similar knack for high finance and a mean layup.

But as her brother had been raised to run the show, Miss Ashley might have been raised to affirm the family's place in high society. Much in the same way Stephanie had been raised. Though the two women seemed to be taking distinctly different paths to that end. Stephanie was out to elevate her family through marriage; Ashley seemed intent on justifying her family's status through good deeds.

Regardless of how they lived their lives, both women apparently considered high fashion the cachet of their status, so Ashley's clothing choices for an afternoon of mountain biking would undoubtedly prove entertaining.

Mac reached up and pulled on the hatch to close it the same moment he heard the front door opening. He glanced back over his shoulder as Ashley emerged from the house.

The hatch hit him on the head.

She was *not* wearing what he'd expected. She had on skimpy black running shorts, a tight black tank top, running shoes and a white sweatshirt draped over one arm. She'd stuffed her blonde locks beneath a black baseball cap. All in all, she looked like a runner. The sculpted muscles in her smooth, tempting thighs that flexed as she bounded down the stairs said serious runner.

Rubbing his sore head, where the hatch hit him, Mac dismissed the notion. She was probably just an aerobics queen. Despite her attire, he couldn't picture Ashley anywhere besides a climate-controlled, mirrored exercise studio.

She approached him with a decidedly challenging swagger more suited to a pro basketball player with *game* and gave him a pointed once-over.

Mac pulled back his chin. May wonders never cease. Not only had she changed in a reasonable amount of time and into somewhat appropriate clothes, but she hadn't lost her surprisingly competitive edge.

Arching her blond brows, she asked, "You ready to go yet?" She said it like she'd been waiting on him.

Damn if she didn't know exactly how to make him like her. Kate had had that *don't give a damn who you are, let's rumble* attitude, also, though she would have never been caught dead in such form fitting attire. She hadn't been comfortable enough in her own skin to show it off with such confidence.

Mac frowned fiercely at the direction of his thoughts. Guilt flared red-hot. He had no business comparing Kate to Ashley. And it didn't matter if he liked Ashley or not.

Keep it casual at the least, physical at the most, MacDougal. That was all he was free to do.

He relaxed his expression and made a show of returning her perusal, then wished he hadn't when it occurred to him how far her running shorts were likely to ride up on the wider, more padded bike seat he'd chosen for her. All too aware of how little his own bike shorts left to the imagination, he cleared his throat and moved to the passenger side of the car. He'd have to make sure he never let her take the lead if he wanted to stay smooth and suave, if he wanted to stay in control.

Opening her door, he said, "I await your pleasure."

She gave a little cough of her own and dropped her gaze, her hesitation before coming toward him and the open car door ratcheting up the physical awareness until it crackled between them.

When she moved to slide into the car, the sweatshirt on her arm shifted and he saw her day planner clutched to her chest. He shook his head. The woman couldn't let go. As confident as she appeared to be about herself, it was weird that she wouldn't step out of her restrictive role. Weird and annoying. He took another long look at her legs as she swung them into the Explorer. Maybe she could be pushed.

"So where to, sunshine?"

Her gaze jerked up and she gave him an odd look. "I'd assumed we were going to familiarize you with the area around the mill."

Mac gave himself a mental head slap. *Environmental Specialist*. "Uh, sure. If you don't mind."

"Of course not. I always try to do whatever I can to help my family's endeavors."

Her bedroom office came to mind. A woman's bedroom was supposed to be a sanctuary. A place to relax and recoup. Who in the hell could relax in a room with a Rolodex the size of a boulder? He looked away at the tidy hedges lining the long, circular driveway and mumbled, "Aren't you the good little girl."

"Pardon me?"

Turning back to her, he said louder, "What about your own endeavors?"

She cocked her head at him, and he couldn't tell if her puzzled look was real or feigned. He waved the question off. "Never mind." He closed her door and went around to the driver's side. Without getting any more interested in Miss Ashley's career choices, he needed to at least make a stab at playing the part Harrison had handed him. If he didn't, she might make it her *endeavor* to figure out what he was up to. He climbed in, started the rig and headed them out.

Between making tour guide-type chitchat about the

area, focusing on environmental issues for his sake, he assumed, and impressing the pleats out of his kilt with her knowledge and sensitivity to the needs of the region, Ashley directed him from the estate toward the mill. According to Ashley, the distance wasn't that great. Apparently the Riverses liked to live close to the cash source.

Since she was so well informed, Mac kept his comments about the flora and fauna as emotion-based, rather than scientifically based, as possible until they reached the hills that alternated between densely forested and clear-cut surrounding the Dover Creek Mill. He was less likely to trip himself up telling her how stirring he found the profound silence of an old growth forest than if he tried to give his opinion of the status of some owl that lived there.

He could feel her stare. He took his eyes off the winding, two-lane highway hugging the McKenzie River long enough to glance at her. She was looking at him like his hair had sprouted pheasant feathers.

"What?"

She blinked at him. "That was very moving, what you just said about a forest's silence."

Prickled by a strange self-consciousness, Mac shifted in his seat. "Yeah, so?"

She looked back at the road, her cheeks pinking. "I...it was...unexpected."

A spurt of concern that he'd already somehow messed up his role shot through him. "Why? Because noticing stuff like that isn't very...scientific?" he risked asking.

"No, not at all. People go into the fields of study

such as yours precisely because of their love of the forests, for the benefits they hold for us all. I was only a bit surprised because my initial impression of you—that is..."

He barked out a laugh, realizing where she was going with her explanation and relieved that he hadn't messed up, after all. "You thought that old Wild Man, here, wasn't the sort to stop and ponder much of anything, let alone silence, didn't you," he accused.

Her blush deepened, and he laughed again.

She shook her head. "No, it's not that—"

"Insulting?" He cocked an eyebrow at her, delighted to have busted her in a social faux pas. But when he saw the distress in her pretty blue-green eyes, he cut her some slack. "It's okay, Ashley. I know what you mean."

She gave him a weak, though definitely grateful smile and fell into silence. Out of the corner of his eye he saw her glancing at him from under the bill of her baseball cap a few times more, probably trying to figure out how a dirty guy on a bike could notice anything besides a finish line. Satisfaction that he'd proven her wrong on that score filled him. He forcefully discounted its significance.

They rounded a bend in the road and Ashley sat forward, pointing ahead. "The turnoff to the mill is right up there."

Afraid he wouldn't be so lucky the next time and would reveal too much of his ignorance if they went to the mill itself, Mac drove past the new-looking sign at the mill yard's entrance, intending to continue on for a few miles.

At her curious look, he offered up the first environmental-sounding thing he could think of. "I want to check erosion factors upstream." He hoped like hell that there was indeed a stream, and that they were heading up it.

The sound of her day planner snapping open drew his attention from the gravel turnout he'd picked to pull off onto.

An excited gleam in her eyes, she said, "I'll take notes for you."

Always the little helper. He sighed and shut off the engine. "No, you just have fun."

"But it would be so much more efficient if you dictate your observations to me—"

Knowing his most likely observation would be *nice butt*, he gave her a stern look. "Ashley. This is just a...a look-see today. You don't have to work for me. Besides, I have an excellent memory."

"If you need to compile data at some point, why not—"

"Ashley, please. Today, fun. Okay?"

She shifted away with what would have been a grumble in a less refined person and started to climb out of the car.

"And the day planner stays."

She stopped and glanced down at the planner she'd clutched to her middle again.

When she hesitated, he added, "How do you expect to ride a mountain bike hanging on to that thing?"

She brightened. "That's easy. I'll tuck it in the back of my waistband and—"

"No. You don't need it. Not today."

He expected her to protest like a baby denied her pacifier, but she raised her chin and regally leaned forward and tucked the planner up under her seat. She fiddled with it for a moment more, probably making sure the sun wouldn't touch it. She then quickly shoved the door open, climbed out with a distinct sniff and slammed the door shut, apparently not able to completely avoid a fit of pique. Thank heaven she was a little human.

By the time he emerged from the car and went to the back to open the hatch, though, she was waiting with a very pleasant and altogether too appealing smile. Maybe getting her to loosen up wasn't such a great idea. Yeah, he was distracted from his problems back home, but maybe a little *too* distracted. She was so gorgeous and smart and annoyingly repressed that if he wasn't careful, he'd tip her off that something was up. He still figured she'd bust him for lying about who he was and tell the whole world where they could find him.

He tried to concentrate on taking the bikes out of the Explorer, but she brushed against him to grab her helmet. Her soft, beckoning scent filled his nostrils. The green flag dropped and his body jumped straight into high gear. At least his hormones didn't have to be reminded to keep it physical.

He couldn't help watching her out of the corner of his eye, expecting her to try to put her helmet on over her baseball hat to keep from exposing less than optimally coifed hair. Instead she pulled the hat from her head and shook out her beautiful, silky blond hair with shampoo commercial flair. All one length and curling under slightly, her hair settled on her creamy shoulders like an enticing golden cloud. His palms burned to slip beneath that soft cloud and trace a path up her graceful neck, to hold her still for his kiss.

His instincts had been right about her hair needing to be freed. Too bad they were the wrong instincts. She was way too pretty with her hair down, softening her and making her as tempting as insider trading to a man with no scruples. Thank the saints he was made of stronger stuff.

Seemingly oblivious to her appeal and with her blue-green eyes sparking with challenge, she clapped her helmet on her head and pronounced, "Let's ride."

ASHLEY'S THIGHS BURNED. But there was no way she was going to fall farther behind Mac on the trail. The uphill path had once been a logging road but was now well-carpeted by grass and small, hardy, maidenhair ferns. The tall, though still slender Douglas fir trees growing thick on either side of the track provided occasional shade, but her exertion, not the sun, had sweat trickling between her breasts and dampening the back of her tank top.

She decided he'd purposefully set the grueling pace up the steady incline to put her in her place for accepting his challenge and for insulting him—though she hadn't meant to. He'd simply surprised her with his moving comment about the forest.

Surprised and intrigued her.

She didn't want to be surprised or intrigued by Mac Wild, so instead of dropping back or asking him to slow down, her competitive juices—the ones she'd had firm command of for years—started flowing and her pride roared to life. A noticer of profound silences or not, he was proving himself to still be a macho man, and she would not let him blow her off as the useless fluff, no, make that the *social secretary* he thought he had her pegged for.

But she had to push herself to keep up. Hopefully the hour she spent running on the treadmill each and every morning would come to her rescue.

She needed to get ahead of him once. Just once. Then she could shove the competitive beast that had threatened her chances of gaining her father's approval, and thus his love, back into the cage where it belonged.

But oh, how she wanted to put Mac in his place, if only for a moment. Then she could return to not being affected by him.

Yeah, right. She gritted her teeth at the mocking voice in her head and pulled her gaze from the hypnotic motion of his beautifully muscled backside. Another excellent reason to get in the lead. The reality of the view from behind Mac was even more enticing than what she'd imagined it would be earlier today. She wasn't the slightest bit happy about it.

He glanced back at her, clearly gauging how close to cardiac arrest she was. She must have looked close. His dark brows slammed together and he sat up straight, guiding his bike with one hand while he paused in his pedaling long enough to let her draw even with him.

"How 'bout we take a break," he offered, not

sounding the least bit winded, his gaze touching on her burning cheeks and her openmouthed breathing.

"We're...almost...to the top," she panted. "We'll stop there."

"But you look like you could use a bre—"

"I can make it to the top, Mac." The beast that had earned her the nickname Ash Bash when she was younger broke completely loose. "And I bet you anything I can get there before you."

His sinfully sexy mouth kicked up on one side. "Anything?"

She glared at him. "Anything."

"You're on, sunshine. And lucky for you, I know CPR." He leaned forward and gripped his handlebars with both hands. "To the top of the ridge, there." He nodded his gleaming, black, aerodynamically sleek helmet toward the spot ahead of them where the logging road narrowed to a single trail, about fifty yards away. "Go!"

Anticipating his signal, she bolted ahead of him, but he quickly regained the distance. Ashley stood up on the pedals and pumped for all she was worth, trading the lead with him with nearly every surge. She knew she had to have the lead, even if only slightly, when the double track ended and became a single hiking trail. He would have to back off, and then there would be no doubt about who had won.

Her heart ready to explode and her vision narrowing, Ashley gave everything she had, but Mac stayed even with her, obviously as focused as she was on being the first to reach the single trail. He began crowding her, his shoulders and elbows bumping hers with each rock of the bikes.

The need to win raged in her blood, and when they reached the narrow trail at the same time, Ashley did the unthinkable. The next time Mac's shoulder came into contact with her own, she lifted her elbow and shoved against the boulder hardness of his biceps. It wasn't much of a shove, but the timing of it was enough to send him flying away from her with a startled, "Hey!"

In a moment of stunning clarity she realized why the logging track had come to an end and led into a single, narrow footpath. They had reached a ridge, and the forest floor dropped away to form a gully on the side closest to Mac. She had just enough time to reach out toward him as he and his bike slipped off the edge.

He tumbled knobby wheels over teakettle down the slope. The sound of high-tech metal and poorly covered flesh crashing through underbrush and breaking branches, mingled with an occasional "oof," reached her over the noise of her ragged breathing.

Ashley skidded to a stop and jumped from her bike, letting it crash to the ground behind her. What had she done?

You've just killed the only man to ever make you feel really alive, that's what.

MAC LAY PERFECTLY STILL for a moment, breathing in the musty smell of decaying needles and trying to separate general, you've-just-fallen-off-a-cliff pain from serious injury. He became concerned about his legs so he cracked an eye open and saw why his feet felt suspended in the air. His heels had come to rest a full leg's length up the trunk of a fir tree. The tree had apparently stopped his downward tumble.

He should be glad, but the agonizing throb in his keister where it had impacted the tree made him feel otherwise. He closed his eye again and let the pain wash over him, lessening with each slow, shallow breath.

He could hear Ashley scrabbling down the slope toward him. He started to yell at her to stay up top, that he was fine, but a fresh wave of pain radiated from his back where something was jabbing into him, and it dawned on him where his bike had ended up. He heaved a sigh of relief. The V frame was stronger than his spine, and since his back wasn't broken, the bike must be okay.

Ashley had almost reached him, her "Don't be dead" pleas growing distinct and downright humorous. He'd laugh later.

She'd actually pushed him off the trail. Miss polite-as-can-be, for-expediency's-sake, no-such-thing-as-a-casual-relationship Ashley had shoved him out of her way. Irrational delight infused him like a painkilling drug. Damn, she was something. He'd known she'd be fiery on the inside; all he'd needed to do was apply a little heat. He made a mental note to never take her rock climbing, though.

The leaf debris from the smaller vine maples he'd crashed through shifted and crunched as she slid to a halt next to him. While he was gratified by the loss of control that proved her human, Mac wasn't inclined to let her off the hook right away. She actually could have killed him.

She hovered above him, begging, "Please, oh please don't be dead."

It took everything he had not to smirk. Killing him would definitely rattle her perfect little cage, certainly more than losing her composure had. While squaring things up was the MacDougal way, making her sweat over what she'd done had its appeal, too. He held himself perfectly still, but when she dropped to her knees next to him, she hit his bike's front fork, driving one of the handlebars into his spleen. He gave an honest groan.

"Oh, thank God. Thank God," she chanted on each huffing breath. "Thank God you're not dead."

Her touch was feather light and quivering on his chest as she apparently checked for broken ribs, then moved to his shoulders and arms. Her touch was erotic because of its innocent intent, and heat started to pool in his groin. When she shifted to check his hips, her fingers spread toward his buttocks and her thumbs pressed down on his pelvic bone, kneading, he thought, *No, but you might just kill me, yet.* Damn these bike shorts, anyway.

On the verge of turning into her touch to give them both a thrill, he lost the opportunity when she let go of his hips and ran her hands up his legs. He grit his teeth as she brushed over various raw scrapes he'd earned on his tumble down before his legs came to rest on the tree trunk.

She took her hands away, and Mac cracked his eyes open to find her poised with her hands reaching toward his ankles, clearly debating whether or not to move his legs.

She dropped her hands, muttering, "No. He might have a broken back. Oh, Lord." She sat back on her haunches, unbuckled her helmet, and yanked it off her head, shoving her sweat-dampened hair away from her face. "Wait. Call 911. That's it." She reached behind her back and pulled a tiny phone and notepad from her waistband.

The stinkpot. She hadn't been positioning her day planner out of the sun, she'd been taking out stuff. So she *still* thought she could outmaneuver him. Well, he knew one sure way to get her mind off being useful and on enjoying life while she could. Before fate, or a narrow, dark highway late at night, took everything away.

"Ashley," he purposefully whined.

She dropped the cell phone she'd been about to dial and turned wide, panicked eyes toward him. "Mac?" She scooted closer toward his head and leaned down near his face. "Oh, Mac, are you all right?" Her pupils were pinpricks of concern, the irises a tangled weave of blue and green with surprising flecks of gold here and there. Heat from exertion radiated from her and added a faint, musky undertone to the delicate, flowery scent of her designer perfume.

Damn, she was pretty. And her concern brought an unexpected warmth to the permafrost residing in his chest. She was so in need of a lesson in living like there was no tomorrow from Wild Man MacDougal.

Keeping his voice a barely audible rasp to draw her yet closer, he said, "I...I will be after...*this*." He shot a hand up and captured the back of her neck, half pulling her down, half rising up to meet her lips with his.

It was meant to be a simple, playful, *ha, gotcha* sort of kiss, but his lips were in contact with hers for barely a second before they were molding together and shifting for a better fit. Next thing he knew he was teasing her lips apart, tasting, testing.

She opened for him with a moan and he took the invitation with everything he had. Her hot, wet tongue met his with a firm, sensual stroke that made his blood roar in his ears and his body surge like an approaching avalanche. The need to cover her with his body, to bury her beneath him, was overwhelming.

He lifted his other hand and burrowed his fingers through the moist silkiness of her hair, gently massaging her scalp. Pulling her deeper into a kiss that already felt dangerously like a bottomless crevasse, he shifted her to the side.

She cupped his face in her hands, her fingers bumping into the underside of his helmet as she alternately stroked his jaw and pulled him closer, like she wanted him to be a part of her.

He nearly exploded. He pulled his legs down from against the tree and started to lift his shoulders, intending to trade places with her so he could fit more closely against her. But the front fork of his bike shifted again and pitched him to the side, putting an abrupt end to the kiss.

Ashley reared back and blinked owlishly at him several times. Then her already flushed face crimsoned more and she made a grab for her cell phone and notepad. "I'm glad you're not dead, Mac" was all she said before she lurched to her feet and scrambled up the slope.

He let his head drop back, his helmet clanking against the undoubtedly bent spokes of his front wheel and repeated his earlier thought out loud. "But you might just kill me, Ashley."

Chapter Six

Ashley glanced out the limousine's window at the front doors again. While the late-afternoon sun glinted nicely off the polished wood of the front doors, there was still no sign of Mac. Pursing her lips, she glared back at the iron lion head door knockers, then checked her watch.

By the time they made it through any remnants of Friday evening traffic on their trip into Eugene, they'd be cutting it close. And since they were mere stand-ins for the true guest of honor, she didn't want to stroll in late.

Donavon busied himself polishing the limousine's already gleaming black hood—the formal car wasn't used frequently enough to warrant a full-time chauffeur—while they waited for Mac to join them. Ashley lowered her window and sat forward. "Donavon, are you sure Mr. Wild was getting ready when you checked on him?"

He raised his dark head and met her gaze with reassuring, soft brown eyes. "He certainly looked to be in the process of getting ready. He said he just needed a few more minutes."

"A few more minutes? More like twenty," Ashley grumbled and sat back.

Maybe Mac had only told Donavon to have her wait in the car to make it easier for him to slip out the back. Hope coiled irrationally with dread in the pit of her stomach. As much as she'd love to get out of having to spend an evening on the arm of the man she'd done her livid best to avoid all week, she couldn't let Grandmother down over something as petty as a stupid little kiss.

She groaned, closed her eyes, and let her head drop back on the gray leather headrest, welcoming the punishing poke of the comb holding her hair tight against her head. That stupid little kiss, which hadn't been little at all, had turned her completely inside out like a too-tight glove. Never in her life had she experienced such a thing. The passion his mouth had ignited that much more devastating for its instantaneousness.

Mac had sidled through a chink in her armor she hadn't previously realized existed. She'd known she was too competitive by half. But she hadn't known she could go up in flames with a simple touching of lips. And tongues. Lord help her, what a feeling. Mac's kiss had been a lightening strike to her core, leaving her feeling hollowed out and altogether singed.

It was bad enough he'd been able to goad her into joining his little game of one-upmanship so easily. And then she herself took it one step further by challenging him to a race...she let out a noisy breath and opened her eyes to stare at the tight nap of the dark-gray felt covering the limo's ceiling.

She'd berated herself all week for allowing Mac

Wild to affect her so much, yet had allowed herself a coward's way out. She'd ignored what had happened on the trip home from the bike ride, not looking at him at all, and had hid in her rooms or left the estate completely to keep from having to face him and whatever she might see in those smoldering tiger eyes. Smugness? Satisfaction? Pity? She pulled in a steadying breath.

Propriety, Presentation and Principle. That's what she should have shown Mac in *her* eyes this week instead of running away. But what was done was done. At least she'd had the sense to send him a card for buying her a bike. His motivation hadn't been flattering, but his effort had been.

While her avoidance tactics hadn't done much for her self-esteem, her shoe collection had benefited nicely. She raised her head to look down at the new, strappy red heels she'd bought that just happened to go quite well with the gown she wore.

She smoothed the red silk over one knee. She loved the simplicity of the dress, nothing much more than a long, modestly cut sheath with spaghetti thin straps, even though she normally preferred a more understated, suitably refined look. Despite how much she liked the dress, she had only worn it one other time.

The night she'd found Roger in bed with another woman.

She'd gone to his apartment, in this dress, to knock his socks off, stupidly hoping to earn a marriage proposal. When he hadn't answered her rap on the door, she'd let herself in with the key she'd never had the spontaneity to use before and followed the sound of voices to his bedroom, thinking they came from the television. What she'd seen and heard before she was spotted standing like a child in the doorway had made her put this dress away forever.

But she'd dug it out of the back of her closet and donned it tonight for a reason. The dress was a potent reminder of the hurt a man could inflict, of how easily she could be used, and would seal up her chinked armor quite nicely.

Shifting her focus to the faint image of herself reflected in the limo's tinted side window glass, she finally admitted there was yet another reason why she'd dressed the way she had. Tonight she wanted to affect Mac at least a little, if not as much, as he affected her. Heaven only knew what the sight of him in the suit she'd bought him would do to her.

Seeing him in the jacket alone the night she'd given it to him had been bad enough. The dark-brown wool had matched the deeper tones in his hair perfectly, and she'd been right in guessing that his broad, muscular shoulders wouldn't need extra padding. He'd looked far too good in the jacket for her peace of mind.

But she'd sworn to hold fast to her control and get through the evening as if nothing had changed since a certain Wild Man had entered her life.

The sound of the heavy front door closing reached the inside of the car and her stomach lurched. Mac came down the steps toward the car, the suit she had bought him looking as perfect on him as she'd expected. That was all that was as she'd expected. She stared slack-jawed as Mac waved off Donavon, who'd moved to open the limo's back door for him.

Mac's hair was oddly combed, parted too far on one side and heavily wetted or slicked down with styling gel, but not all the way to the ends, which he'd left dry and curling. And he wore black-framed glasses with small, rectangular lenses. The topper, though, was the bits of tissue stuck here and there to bloody nicks on his chin, jaw, and throat. Since she assumed that a man as well supplied in testosterone as Mac would have been shaving for the majority of his life, the fact that he could still cut himself so much had her frowning in concern.

He opened the door himself and gave her only a slight nod as he climbed into the car and stepped over her legs to sit on her other side. He settled himself in the seat, fastened his seat belt, then finally looked at her as Donavon got them on their way.

"What?" he asked, his tone defensive and his usually glowing eyes banked, with not so much as a trace of the smug knowing she'd feared all week.

Ashley blinked a few times to regain her wits and tried to excuse her rudeness. "I...I didn't know you wore glasses."

"Oh. Well, yeah. Though not much. Contacts, mostly. I, ah, lost one. That's what took me so long. Sorry."

A disconcerting rush of pleasure that he hadn't been simply considering standing her up so he wouldn't have to face her after their kiss warmed her. She quelled it with a hearty dose of purpose and reached for her red silk handbag. If she could shove Mac back into the niche of being just another person she did things *for,* not *with,* life would return to normal.

She pulled out her miniplanner. "Do you have your vision correction prescription? Or at least your eye doctor's name? I can get you a new set of contacts delivered to the house." Out of the corner of her eye she saw him shoot her planner a glance as she made a note to herself:

New contacts for Mr. Wild.

He made a rude noise. "I'll handle it, Ash."

His shortening her name sounded so much more intimate than when her brother or sister-in-law did it. Her cheeks heated, making her latch onto irritation like a life preserver in high seas. She closed her planner with more force than necessary. "Why won't you let me help you?"

He let out a distinctly long-suffering breath. "Because I don't need your help, okay?"

His dismissal hit her like a crushing blow. "Just because you don't need it doesn't mean you can't accept it."

He turned in his seat to face her, glaring at her over the top of his ridiculously small glasses. "Now that's just silly," he said, throwing back at her the words she had used to discount the notion that she owed him. "Why should you have to do things for me that I don't need?"

Because it makes me feel worthwhile.

Instead of telling him the truth, she raised her chin and rebutted, "Because I can."

The pestered look slipped from his face and one of his wonderful, wicked eyebrows twitched upward slightly. A faint smile touched his sensuous mouth as his gaze, glowing again with his own brand of heat, drifted downward over her suddenly too-thin dress with the impact of a touch. "I'm discovering you can do all sorts of things, sunshine."

Her body responded as if they had kissed only a moment ago, not a week. Fighting in desperation for her equilibrium, she focused on the bit of toilet paper plastered to his chin by a dried drop of blood. "I certainly could have given you a better shave."

His expression shifted yet again, as if her reminder had brought him back to his own reality. He raised a big, tan hand and probed gently at the spot with a blunt fingertip, testing the tissue's readiness to be removed. "Yeah, well, I'm not exactly my usual self tonight."

Far more concerned than she should be, Ashley pressed, "How so?"

He faced forward and shrugged, but when he yanked off the rest of the tissues, checked the horrendous lay of his hair with light pats, and straightened his glasses until they were crooked, realization dawned on Ashley like the blazing summer sun.

"I don't suppose you have much call to attend formal charity functions in your line of work, do you, Mac?"

He smirked in a very self-deprecating way. "There aren't too many black-tie stream reclamation grand openings held these days, no."

She put a hand lightly on his thigh, ignoring through sheer strength of will the slight flex of his muscle with its resulting hardness and the heat warming the finely made brown wool beneath her palm. She softened her voice. "There's no need to be nervous, Mac. The people who are honoring Grandmother tonight are some of the kindest, most generous people I have the pleasure of knowing. You'll do fine."

He nodded, shifted on the leather seat, and readjusted his long legs.

She self-consciously removed her hand from his leg, her palm hot and tingling.

He didn't seem to notice, directing his attention out the window at the increasing traffic and development as they left little Plainview behind and drew nearer to the city of Eugene. He sat silently for a while, but the pulse of life and strength radiating from him let her know he wasn't anywhere near being reassured, let alone relaxed.

Finally he murmured, "I don't want to do your family a disservice by calling attention to myself."

Ashley's heart exploded with compassion and empathy. Never in her wildest dreams would she have thought a man like Mac Wild capable of insecurity. Maybe his *omelets with a pretty girl* routine was just that, a routine to cover for not knowing how to act in a place like the Rivers's estate, to make up for feeling unsure of himself. She ached with the thought, memories of her own fears of never earning approval, of never being able to contribute, far too close to the surface.

She returned her hand to his leg, and he turned to look at her, his topaz gaze hooded and unreadable. She squeezed his hard thigh in reassurance. "You don't have a thing to worry about, Mac. I'll help you."

He closed his eyes and made a rumbling sound deep

in his broad chest, then raised a hand and slid his thumb and forefinger beneath his glasses to pinch the bridge of his nose. "That's exactly what I'm afraid of."

Not the least deterred, but unsure of how to handle how drawn she was to this new side of Mac, Ashley released her grip on his leg, giving it one last, just-friends type of pat before settling back in her seat. In a world where confidence and acceptance were everything, she could relate to his uncertainty, but the mutual need to fit in bonded them in a way she found uncomfortable.

He settled the little black glasses back on his nose and glanced at her. Softly he said, "Oh, and hey, thanks for the thank-you card. For the bike. You didn't have to, you know. Especially the mailing part."

Warmed to her toes by the honesty in his gaze and his persistence—this time gentle—of what she shouldn't feel compelled to do, she smiled at him. "Yes, I did. It was sweet of you to buy it for me."

He looked away and cleared his throat. "Yeah, well, it was my pleasure." Looking back at her, the heat in his golden brown eyes trapped the breath in her lungs. "All of it."

For a moment, she thought he might kiss her again. She swore she could see the memory of their last kiss in his eyes. But he instead looked forward at Donavon, then shifted his attention back outside. Pulling in several deep breaths, she fought to regain her equilibrium. Thank goodness he'd apparently realized this wasn't exactly a private moment.

While she now had real reasons to fear that the big,

sensual man next to her might slip past the additional armor her red dress provided, she also suddenly had serious doubts about the strength of the mortar and stone protecting what was left of her heart.

MAC SLIPPED FARTHER INTO the shielding fronds of the giant palm plant, chanting softly, "Be the plant, become the plant."

Looking between the long, slender, light-green fronds, he watched the postbanquet smooze-fest that was in full swing amongst the dozens of large, round, white linen and crystal swathed tables scattered about the hotel ballroom with a wary eye. In the muted light from the dimmed chandeliers hung high above their heads, he hadn't recognized any of the guests, but that didn't mean one or two might not know him on sight. Especially with the attention he'd received from the *entertainment* media after Stephanie had started dropping hints that he'd seduced her and knocked her up.

He snorted. She should live so long.

His gaze landed on Ashley in her red dress and his mouth went dry. *He* should live so long. Getting a chance to take her to bed would be worth the wait, if the kiss they'd shared was any indication of what lovemaking would be like between them. He pulled his chin back at the unexpected thought, but didn't have time to try to dismiss it because he realized Ashley was looking for him.

Not ready to face her right after thinking such disconcerting thoughts, he tried to become part of the plant again.

He knew the second it ceased working when Ashley's searching gaze halted on him, her eyes lighting with success. She'd chase him down if he made a run for it, so he accepted his fate for the moment and waited with his hands shoved into his pockets for her to weave her way through the clusters of chatting Armani and sequins until she reached him.

She'd been like Patton in Africa, confident atop her mighty tank of impeccable manners and endless connections, in her quest to make him feel comfortable and welcome among what he assumed to be the big fish of the charity set in this part of the country. Thank the god of good bagpipes none he'd been forced to meet so far migrated at all to his family's ponds.

But the night was still young. He could still get busted for the liar he was.

They'd arrived late enough to have missed the predinner cocktail hour, and he'd been able to keep his head down over his plate during the meal, tempted to look up only by the sound of Ashley's startlingly rich laughter. Women like her usually had a molar-grinding titter.

Not his challenge-issuing, elbow-throwing, hot-kissing Ash. Man, she'd tossed him for a loop. Fortunately she'd sent him that thank-you card and jolted some sense into him. He'd done his damnedest to avoid passing her ship in the night while sailing the halls of the Rivers estate since then. But he hadn't been able to come up with an idea to get out of coming with her to Dorothy's banquet.

During the dinner, he hadn't been surprised by the praise heaped on the Rivers family by those at their table. Harrison had seemed the type clear back in college. And talk of their charitable pursuits had kept the focus off her escort, despite Ashley's attempts to draw him into the conversations.

Mac had managed to excuse himself to the rest room when the time came to present Ashley with her grandmother's award, but the Master of Ceremony's words and Ashley's praise of Dorothy's work had reached him. A prickle of guilt for not doing more with his own wealth and connections had surprised him as he'd made his way to the potted plants in the corner to wait out the remainder of the evening, which threatened to last even longer when a band started to play.

Maybe when the mess with Stephanie blew over he'd look into contributing more to the MacDougals' charities. He knew there were some, he'd just never given them much thought.

Kate certainly would have.

The day they met, she'd been tearing across campus on her bike, late for her volunteer shift at the clinic, when he'd stepped out in front of her. Being the caring sort beneath her rough and tumble veneer, she'd insisted on nursing his bruises, and then went on to spend the next three years goading him into experiencing life outside of Harvard Business.

That collision had forever changed the way he lived his life. But perhaps not enough.

His insides seized and twisted as they always did when he realized he was still failing her. And he hadn't thought of her in days.

He needed a drink. But Ashley had spotted him.

As she wove her way toward him, her dress alternately clung and flowed around her like red mercury, hinting at what lay beneath. He had no choice but to acknowledge his admiration for her. She was certainly made up of more than he'd first given her credit for. Stunning beauty, classic manners, faultless generosity and a competitive streak a mile wide.

When she reached him, she wore a genuine smile.

He had to lock his knees.

"Mac! You look lost in the shrubbery! Come on out and join the fun." She latched onto his arm the second she came close enough.

His urge to bolt must have shown. Or maybe she found his nerd look irresistible. He'd done his Jimmy-best to alter his looks as much as he could without drawing Ashley's suspicions. But why he'd thought his golly-shucks-ain't-never-been-to-town routine would get her to let him hang in a corner, safe from the risk of meeting someone he might know, was beyond him. It should have occurred to him that she'd pounce on the chance to help him as she would the most deserving of charities. Someone was bound to recognize him at this rate.

She was treating him like the poster child for the socially disabled. Something he most definitely was not. He'd been weaned on functions twice this size, wearing a kilt, no less, as that was considered formal attire in his family.

And speaking of attire, he couldn't take Ashley Rivers in a slinky red dress much longer before he pounced on her like a starving wolf on an unsuspecting lamb. The memory of their kiss, of the way her hot mouth had felt beneath his, was too close to the surface. His body was constantly primed for contact with hers.

She tucked his arm close to her curvy body to entice him away from the plants filling the corner of the large ballroom and his head nearly popped off his shoulders.

He'd thought for sure she wouldn't look at him, let alone champion him, after he'd stupidly laid one on her last weekend. Especially considering the way she'd made herself scarce since then, going as far as *mailing* her thank-you card to him. Maybe she thought it didn't count unless it was postmarked. Still, her avoiding him had been the best thing for them both.

He couldn't help glancing at her cleavage as she pulled him out of the corner. She might have decided to dress like a goddess and torture him with wanting what she wasn't about to let him have. That made sense.

Then he'd shown up looking like a dork, and her powers of pity seemed to have overcome her need to avoid him. Damn it. He couldn't win.

He had no choice but to let her escort him into the fray, feeling every eye in the place touching on them repeatedly. Ashley was simply too beautiful not to draw attention. Where there wasn't red silk there was flawless skin, making him want to run his hands from her graceful neck exposed by her upswept, fair hair all the way down to her red polish-tipped toes.

Hopefully no one would look too closely at the geek on her arm.

The thought had no sooner formed than he spotted a man with a professional-looking camera and flash unit heading for them.

Mac bit back a curse.

Ashley had come to a stop behind a short, black-haired woman in a dress so beaded it looked like chain mail and was about to tap the woman on the shoulder. Mac leaned down and put his mouth close to her ear, unconsciously burrowing his nose into her soft, flowery smelling hair. He let his lips graze the sensitive skin of her delicate ear, enjoying her sharp intake of breath. "Let's dance."

Ashley froze, her hand suspended midair over the other woman's shoulder.

The flash of a camera strobe lit the world.

Without taking his nose from Ashley's hair, Mac looked toward the photographer out of the corner of his eye. The camera had been aimed at them.

Damn it. The jig was up now. Not only would Ashley learn the truth when he was identified in the photo, but his family and Stephanie would find out where he was.

Seeming oblivious to the fact that they had just had their picture taken, or perhaps so used to it at these functions she didn't react, Ashley leaned away and glanced up at him. "Dance?" She looked toward the front of the room where there were indeed couples slow dancing to the low-keyed, bluesy music. Her eyes were wide when she returned her gaze to his. "You and me?"

His heart squeezed tight at how right those words sounded coming from her lips. "Yeah. You and me."

He took a quick glance at the photographer who appeared about ready to hail them, undoubtedly to ask Mac's name for the caption if the paper used the picture. And since Ashley was, in essence, the guest of honor, the odds were high the photo would be run. A picture of the honoree with a man attached to her ear would be far more interesting than one of her holding a boring old plaque.

Especially when that man turned out to be Wilder Huntington MacDougal V, the heir to one of the oldest fortunes in the country and stinking rich in his own right. Not to mention the fact that he was on the cusp of a very juicy scandal that would interest other papers, thanks to Stephanie's lies. Lies he should have learned from. He knew Ashley well enough by now to realize how hurt she'd be once she learned the truth about him. How things would change forever between them.

This would be Mac's last chance to get close to Ashley Rivers, and he was going to take it. "Come on."

Without giving her time to think about it, Mac pulled her past the small clusters of people and wove between the round tables that were still partially occupied by those lingering over their desserts and conversations. He put as many couples as possible between them and the photographer, undoubtedly a photojournalist for the society page, before he swung her into his arms.

The second he placed his hand on the small of her back and met her wide, upturned gaze Mac knew he'd made a tactical error. The sparks shooting off the points where his body grazed hers, with only a thin layer of red silk and summer-weight brown wool between them, would certainly draw attention. The photo probably wouldn't appear until the Sunday edition of the paper, which would give him another full day to figure out what to do, but if someone recognized him on the spot tonight, that would be the end of his apparently not so brilliant plan.

Ashley fell into step with the motion he'd set, tilting her hips against his, and he ceased to care.

Whether she'd done it on purpose or not didn't matter. Mac acknowledged that he really, really liked having Miss Ashley Rivers in his arms. And since he would have her there only temporarily, he refused to waste his time considering what a bad thing his liking her there was.

Seeming to get over the shock of him wanting to dance, she said, "Now, tonight hasn't been so bad, has it, Mac?"

He grunted in response, not wanting to delve any deeper into his behavior. He hadn't even been able to flat out lie to her about why he'd changed his appearance. He *didn't* want to do a disservice to her family by calling attention to himself, but not for the reasons she'd assumed. He wasn't socially inept, he was socially infamous thanks to Stephanie Thorton-Stuart and her lies. The Rivers family didn't deserve to have their name linked with Wilder MacDougal V right now, despite what Dorothy might think.

Obviously realizing his surviving the night wasn't the best subject for conversation, Ashley narrowed her eyes and tilted her head in a thoughtful look. "You know, I think larger lenses would suit your face more." She lifted her hand from where she'd rested it featherlight on his shoulder and touched the tip of the black frames. "These are much too small. As a matter of fact, I think grandmother has a pair just like these."

He suppressed a wry smile. They were *exactly* like these, since he'd swiped them on his way out to the limo from the side table in the library where she'd left them with her embroidery. Hopefully his fat head hadn't stretched them out too much. But since it was Dorothy's fault he was playing Clark Kent in the first place, loose reading glasses were a small price for her to pay.

He grunted again in response. Okay, so he *had* lied to her. He didn't need glasses or contacts. But knowing Ashley—and the fact that he *did* know her after such a short time made him blink—he'd probably have to start wearing one or the other because she'd see to it that he had a new pair by the end of the day tomorrow.

His cavemanesque conversation style had her heaving a sigh and settling back into silence, her hand returning to his shoulder.

He flexed his hand on the small of her back and drew her closer.

She complied and fit herself against him, letting her head rest against the front of his shoulder. They matched up perfectly, as if they'd been made for each other. Mac closed his eyes at the useless thought and breathed her delicate, designer scent in deeply, letting it settle in his memory for later torture.

The intimacy of their embrace worked great at keeping the other couples from talking to them, but even if it hadn't, Mac was in no hurry to change a thing.

He'd be returning to his romantically sterile existence soon enough.

They moved together song after song, the music lulling them into a rhythm as natural as the way she felt in his arms. He hadn't felt this good, this content, with a woman in a very long time. Which surprised him considering how explosive their kiss had been. It worried him to think he could have both passion and tenderness with her. So much for keeping it physical.

And she'd hate him when she learned the truth, and her hate would be another wound on his heart, another aching scar to bear for the rest of his life.

Another scar he deserved.

Chapter Seven

Ashley's fantasy ended with the music.

For the too short time she and Mac had been on the dance floor, swaying to their own music, the band's melodies a mere backdrop, she'd let herself pretend. She'd pretended that her heart was whole and that Mac Wild wanted it.

He'd certainly held her as if he had, clutching her close like a treasure, making her feel cherished for the woman she was, not for whose family she represented or the size of her trust fund.

The grip of his hand as he held hers was gentle but sure, and the hand he'd nestled against the small of her back held her tight against him, occasionally flexing his strong fingers possessively. While her body throbbed with awareness of his as they swayed together, there was such comfort and rightness in the contact it lulled her into a magical place. A place she'd only dreamt about sharing with a man. A place she'd come to fear she'd never reach. She was so thankful toward Mac for taking her there at least once.

But when the music ended, she immediately pulled away. To linger in his arms would be bad form. And here, amongst her father's friends and associates, the Three P's drilled into her at prep school were especially important. They were what had made her so successful in these types of situations, what had made her father so proud.

She stepped out of Mac's arms. The residue of her fantasy made her whole body feel flushed and her eyes naked, so she only met his gaze briefly as they trailed off the dance floor with the last stragglers.

"Thank you, Mac. For the dance, for tonight, for everything. I know it wasn't easy for you, but I had a wonderful time because of you."

He reached up and gripped her elbow, his fingers warm and strong. The consistent possessiveness of his touch thrilled her. No man had ever made her feel the way he did; electrified knowing he wanted her, a heady certainty that he would make her feel worshiped.

"You're welcome, Ash. And you were right. It wasn't so bad."

"See, I told you—"

He leaned close to cut her off. "Mostly because I had the chance to hold you in my arms."

Before she could decide if he was simply being complimentary out of politeness or if the shadows darkening his topaz gaze held something more, something closer to what she was feeling, she had to step ahead of him to avoid the waiters scrambling to clear the dozens of large, round tables. But she had no doubt that there was something between them. Something very real, very compelling and very dangerous.

She focused again on making her way toward their

table to retrieve her grandmother's plaque. Only Mr. and Mrs. Breckinridge remained at the table, but they, too, were preparing to leave. Though more the age of her father, they were dear friends and charity cohorts with her grandmother.

Ashley gave the stout woman a hug, careful not to dislodge Mrs. Breckinridge's black satin wrap or muss her tightly curled, graying blond hair. "It was delightful getting to see you, Bea."

"You, too, sweetheart." She returned Ashley's hug, then stepped back and gestured to her tall, slender husband, looking much improved after his bypass surgery. "Jack and I were just commenting on how wonderful it is to see you finally tending to your own enjoyment, and not just that of others. You and your young man make a gorgeous pair, you know. You two looked made for each other out there on the dance floor."

Ashley's heart started to pound and she struggled to keep the panic that surged through her veins from showing on her face. Other people had noticed how much she'd let her guard down with Mac? What had she been thinking?

You weren't thinking at all, you were feeling. For the first time in years.

Ashley's blood raced with the realization and nervous excitement nearly overwhelmed her.

But it was time to get back to reality. She pulled in a calming deep breath. These were her father's friends. She couldn't let them believe that her head could so easily be turned from her goal. She was still the mannerly, devoted daughter her father had once thought her incapable of being. She hadn't gone off on her own. She *was* as capable as Harrison and could contribute to the family.

Too afraid to look at Mac and the temptation he represented, she laughed lightly and waved a hand at him, accidentally hitting his chest. She turned the motion into a pat.

He captured her hand in one of his and held it tight against the steady, strong beat of his heart. It was one of the most intimate gestures she had ever experienced.

Ashley nearly lost the capacity to speak. "Oh, heavens. Mac's the sort to make any partner he chooses look like she belongs. He's quite the dancer."

Jack leaned in. "Able to sweep pretty women off their feet, eh?" He gave them a wink and his wife a nudge. "We'd better let these two be on their way before the night's gone, Bea. Ashley, tell your grandmother we said hello and congratulations. Mac, it was good to meet you."

Mac murmured a return sentiment, picked up the gold-and-black plaque off the table, and indicated for Ashley to precede him out of the ballroom.

Due to the additional goodbyes she had to say on their way to the car, she didn't have the opportunity to gauge Mac's reaction to what the Beckinridges had said. Probably for the better. She had failed miserably in her bid to be unaffected by Mac.

So miserably, in fact, she feared she was falling for him.

The thought settled on her chest like the leaden weight of her father's disapproval.

The red dress had backfired and the wall of mortar

and stone around her heart turned to dust. She had never felt more vulnerable in her life. And she had no idea what to do about it.

AFTER DONAVON'S INITIAL quizzing about the state of health and happiness of those in attendance that he knew, the ride back to the estate was blessedly quiet and quick. While there were a few subtle differences in Mac's behavior on the way home compared to on the way to the banquet—he leaned toward her rather than away, allowing his knee to rest against hers, and more glances were made in her direction—he didn't say much of anything. He seemed as lost in his thoughts as she was in hers.

Did he regret their new closeness? Did he still feel unsure of himself? The idea tore at her heart in a way she hadn't thought possible after Roger's betrayal. Given the walled-up, battered heap Roger had left her heart, so much of what she felt seemed impossible. Maybe she was wrong about what she was feeling. Maybe she'd confused lust and charm and flattery with real, potentially damaging emotions.

She didn't know what to think or do. When she'd found Roger in bed with that woman, had heard his plan, she'd known exactly what to do. To protect her family, she had to sever all ties with Roger as completely and as quietly as she could. All the while secretly wanting to rip his throat out.

Since he hadn't wanted to be publicly labeled a gold digger any more than she wanted to be exposed as a near victim of one, he had agreed to help her lead everyone to believe that they had simply grown apart.

No one had suspected a thing. No one had pressed her for details. And above all else, there had been no doubt.

Tonight, doubt was all she had.

They arrived home before she'd come close to sorting through her feelings.

Falling back on good manners, she turned to Mac as she waited for Donavon to open her door. "Thank you again, Mac, for tonight. I am so grateful to you for doing this for Grandmother."

The car door opened and Donavon offered her his hand, helping her out of the car. Mac climbed out behind her and escorted her up the steps to the house, his hand warm, sure, and achingly familiar on her bare arm.

"You're welcome. But I didn't do it for Dorothy."

She glanced at his face as he ushered her into the foyer, but the huge crystal chandelier hung high above had been dimmed and she couldn't see his meaning in his eyes. "Then why?"

Donavon leaned in through the front door behind them. "Excuse me," he begged of them both. "Is there anything else I can do for you tonight?"

Ashley gave Mac a questioning look, but he was already shaking his head at Donavon. She added her answer. "No, nothing. Thank you for driving us."

The older man smiled warmly at her. "My pleasure. I'll put the car away, and see you tomorrow. Good night."

"Good night, Donavon," she returned as he closed the door.

Mac shifted beside her, his big body giving off a

beckoning heat and sensual scent of spice and man. Being alone with him was not the best place for her with her emotions so unsettled. As much as she'd like to hear his reasons for attending the function tonight, she needed to put distance between them. She was too attracted to him, too close to the brink of her control.

She started backing toward the stairs. "And I'll see you tomorrow, too. I'm afraid I'm done in. A little too much, er, excitement, I suppose."

He lowered his brows slightly. "Oh." Then he nodded. "Yeah, all right. Good night, then."

She hesitated. Was that disappointment she heard in his voice? The prospect exhilarated and terrified her at the same time. But she couldn't take such a drastic step in her life while harboring so much uncertainty.

With a tremulous and far too self-conscious smile she said, "Good night." She waved stupidly as she started up the stairs, mounting them quickly so he wouldn't be close behind her when she reached the top. A left turn to reach her rooms, a right to reach his. It probably wouldn't take much effort on his part to get her to...she shut down the thought. No. Not tonight.

Then when? the newly awakened and aching, lonely part of her asked.

She slipped her little red purse off her shoulder with the intent of getting out her miniplanner, then stopped herself. No matter how tempting it was to simply pencil Mac in, she couldn't schedule a relationship.

Or could she?

She pulled in a settling breath and turned toward her rooms. She desperately needed to think. To decide on a course of action that would give her much-needed peace.

And she knew of only one place she could count on being able to think, one place where perhaps the memory of Mac Wild's seductive lure couldn't influence her.

AN HOUR LATER, Mac hesitated in the hall outside Ashley's door. He could raise his hand and knock, or he could continue on down the hall toward the backstairs to the pool as he'd intended. Or had he decided to go for a late-night swim simply because he had to pass by her room to get to the pool?

No, he'd decided to take a swim because he seriously needed to soak his head. Holding Ashley on the dance floor...that had pushed some buttons that even their knockout kiss hadn't come close to pushing. The kiss had been about sex. Really, really great sex, but just sex, nonetheless. There was no doubt how good it would be between them.

He'd thought that's what it would be about on the dance floor, too. But when Ashley had relaxed against him and rested her head on his shoulder, alarm bells should have gone off and his normally highly effective defenses should have slammed into place. They hadn't. Holding Ashley in his arms, moving with her to the music, had just felt good.

Mac didn't want to feel good with another woman that way. He wouldn't allow himself that luxury.

Because of Kate.

He had made an oath to her on her deathbed, and he wouldn't break it. Regardless of the cost to himself.

Besides, it had been stupid to mess with Ashley as much as he had already. She could be nothing more than a fling, and no matter how much she may need, and even want, to live it up a little with him, she was Harrison's sister, for saint's sake. He owed his friend more consideration than that.

He turned away from her door and continued down the hall, making a conscious effort to walk quietly in his soccer slides. He went down the back stairs to the door to the pool, entering the code he'd been given on the security touch pad and letting himself out.

Though it was well past midnight, the pool light was on and the security lighting near the detached garage provided more than enough illumination to see by. The crystalline aqua water in the large, rectangular pool shimmered and steamed in the night air, beckoning him.

He dropped his towel onto a chaise lounge and started to peel off the white T-shirt he'd pulled on in deference to the night chill, but a whacking and thumping sound coming from the other side of the huge laurel hedge surrounding the pool drew his attention. He realized the lights actually were coming from the basketball court he'd killed time on during the past week. Maybe Donavon hadn't been able to sleep, either. Mac seriously doubted the guy had been lying awake thinking about Ashley and her red dress, however. At least he better not have.

Mac straightened his shirt and with purposeful strides headed for the break in the hedge past the end of the pool.

He emerged at the end of the sport court just as a

basketball *swooshed* through the hoop. Nothing but net. Only it wasn't the lanky butler who had nailed the two points.

It was Ashley Rivers, with her hair in a sporty ponytail and dressed in an oversize, red-and-black Portland Trail Blazers tank top, loose, black mesh shorts—that showed off her great legs—and her running shoes. She stood at the top of the key in the classic star-athlete pose with arms raised, wrists loose, and one toe turned slightly in.

Mac's jaw dropped.

She caught sight of him and started. "Good heavens, Mac. You scared me. What are you doing here?"

He blew out an incredulous breath and ran his hand through his hair, still damp from the shower he'd taken to wash out the gel and to try to cool his head. The woman was turning out to be a whole bundle of surprises. "I was just about to ask you the same thing."

She turned her gaze to the basketball rolling across the court toward Mac's feet. "Nothing. I'm not doing anything."

"Well, you're *nothing* was all net." He bent and scooped up the ball. "Bet you can't do it again." He held the ball with two hands in front of his chest, ready to bounce pass it to her.

Tucking her hands behind her back, she shook her head so hard her ponytail hit her in the face. "I'm not betting you anything ever again, Mac Wild. And I don't play basketball."

Mac pulled a face and threw the ball to her anyway. She reflexively caught it like a pro.

He smirked, wondering what in the hell was up. "Could have fooled me. Sink another one."

She turned the ball over and over in her hands, then shook her head again, her full mouth curving down at the corners.

Drawn to her like she had him on a belaying rope, Mac moved to her side. He could tell she'd been at it for a while by the fine sheen of perspiration on her skin that heated her perfume from its earlier subtlety to a sensual calling card. His body immediately responded to the chemical party invite.

Her miserable expression had him putting his libido on hold. Concern for her grabbing hold of his chest and squeezing, he leaned to catch her evasive gaze. "You want to tell me what's up, Ash?"

She made a noise he'd never expected to hear from her. "Do you realize that you are the only one other than Harrison and Juliet to shorten my name like that?" She snorted again. "I can't believe how much it gets to me."

Jolted by distress for unwittingly upsetting her, Mac quickly offered, "I'm sorry. I didn't realize you don't care for it. I'll stop."

"No. It's not that I don't like it." She glanced at him, then looked back at the ball before he could tell what she was feeling. "Just the opposite."

She toyed with the ball in her hands a little more, and Mac kept silent, sensing there was more to come, intrigued as hell by what else this surprising woman could reveal to him. And how much more dangerous she might become as a result.

"Do you know what Harrison called me when we were teenagers?"

He raised a brow. "Not Ash?"

She gave him a wry smile and started tossing the ball in the air and catching it, apparently not the least concerned about her perfect manicure. "He always called me Ash Bash."

While the memory of her well-placed elbow knocking him off the bike trail flashed through his brain, the need to know everything about her had him repeating, "Ash Bash?"

She nodded, her gaze solemn.

"Dare I ask why?"

She let the basketball drop to the ground and began deftly dribbling it. "Because I was the only one who could drive him off the ball." She illustrated by bending slightly at the waist then sending her shoulder up and into him, knocking him off balance and forcing him back a step. She caught the ball middribble and launched it at the hoop.

Nothing but net. Damn, she was good.

He planted his hands on his hips. "I hate to disillusion you, sunshine, but that would be playing basketball. Quite successfully, I might add."

She stood with her arms loose at her sides, her gaze down. "I know. I always had a real knack for it. But I haven't touched a ball in fifteen years."

Mac hesitated. He shouldn't delve any deeper, shouldn't find out more about this woman who already tugged at him in a way he hadn't experienced since Kate.

The sorrow in her tone and the defeat in her posture

made him ignore the warning and ask anyway. "Why?"

"Because of the way I pursued the game. My complete focus on it made my dad think I was too competitive, too independent, to be a contributing member of our family." She let her head drop back and stared up at the blackness above, exposing the creamy length of her graceful neck.

The slender muscles in her throat flexed and her full breasts rose as she pulled in a shuddering breath before she continued. "He'd always assumed I'd go off on some sports scholarship and do my own thing, so he never included me in any of the plans he made for the family's corporate interests." She lowered her gaze and met his, her eyes shimmering in the floodlights. "I didn't want to be shut out, Mac. I wanted to be a part of what my family does. I have the same drive to contribute, to continue the legacy, as Harrison does, and I wanted my father to feel he could depend on me also."

The tug on his insides became a yank that sent all sorts of barriers crashing down. He stepped near her again and said softly, "So you killed Ash Bash."

One corner of her gorgeous mouth kicked up. "I guess you could say that."

"And with the death of Ash Bash came the birth of Miss Manners."

She blinked hard, clearing her eyes, and straightened her posture from that of a slightly pigeon-toed athlete to a regal lady. "I chose to be what my father could depend on. Especially after my mother died."

Regretting her retreat and hating her self-induced

emotional incarceration as much as he was starting to hate his own, Mac challenged, "A rigid, repressed Miss Prim who never has any fun?"

Her chin shot up. "I have fun."

"Shopping doesn't count. I'm talking about grown-up fun. You know, like dating."

He reached up a hand and ran a finger over the damp, warm skin on her bare shoulder. She gave an apparently irrepressible shudder and his body shouted, *Game on!*

Lowering his voice a notch, he added, "And *sex*. Just plain, old-fashioned, for the hell of it sex." When she started to protest more he held up his hands. "Hey, you told me yourself you don't believe in casual relationships."

"I don't."

"Okay, fine. But when was the last time you had a *serious* relationship, complete with all the contact sports that go with it?"

She looked away. "Six years ago."

Part of him leapt with possessive satisfaction that she'd gone so long without being involved with any man but him. The other part was stunned by such proof of her unwillingness to get involved, of all that time spent without emotional or physical release. "Six years. Wow. No wonder you're wound so tight."

Her lack of reaction worried him further. He continued to push her to talk. "And that one ended because…?"

"We wanted different things."

He thought of Stephanie and all the very specific things she wanted, namely his name and access to his bank account. He nodded in understanding. "A common enough reason."

"After that relationship...ended, it became clear to me what my life should be about. What I should make my focus."

He held up a finger, his indignation over her sacrifices resurfacing. "Let me guess, being indispensable to your family."

"Correct."

Mac crossed his arms over his chest and struggled for composure. "So you're willing to repress your true self. To not live the life you're capable of living. To not allow yourself to find out where a casual relationship might lead."

"Yes."

All his earlier thoughts about what he was allowed and who he shouldn't mess with got zapped like the night insects drawn to the floodlights shining on the court. He needed to go down this road tonight with this woman. She desperately needed him to, whether she'd admit it or not. And damn it, he wanted to be the one along for the ride, even if it had to be a short one.

He uncrossed his arms and closed the distance between them, crowding her until her scent filled his head with an ominous buzz. Her curves drew him closer still. "But relationships can be so much fun, Ashley. No—" He stopped himself and raised a hand to cup her satiny cheek. The smoothness of her skin made his body ache to feel the rest of her. "You're Ash Bash tonight. You've already brought her back from the dead, so why not let her live a little."

The air around them crackled with the energy of a summer storm. He knew he should head for cover, but he had a feeling this would be the kind of light show most people never get the chance to experience in their lives. And damn if he didn't feel like dancing in a metal rowboat with a lightning rod. He teased her full lips with his thumb.

Her eyes closed. "I can't, Mac. I'm not that girl anymore."

The need in her voice pierced his gut, making him sure that both of them should have this night together. Both of them could be selfish just this once.

"No, you're not that girl. You're a woman. A woman who has the right to live for herself once in a while." He raised his other hand and trapped her face, willing her to understand through the heat of his touch. "God, Ashley, life can be so damn short." He closed his eyes and the image of Kate's pale, lifeless hand in his bombarded him. He had to gasp for his next breath. She'd been so young, so full of potential.

And he'd let her down.

He opened his eyes and searched Ashley's tangle of blues and greens for understanding, for an anchor to stop his own drifting.

She reached up and put a hand over his heart. He pulled one hand from her face and trapped her hand to his chest, holding it against him like he'd done at the banquet to reassure her. Only now she was reassuring him.

Mac made his decision. Come Sunday morning, she'd hate him for it, for compounding his lies with intimacy, but he needed to be with Ashley—wanted this physical connection. It was all he could offer. All he could accept.

He moved closer yet until her breasts pressed against his chest and her belly contacted his heat. "You can't let life pass you by. You deserve to live it while you can. Let me show you what you've been missing, Ash. Just for as long as I'm here. Then when I'm gone, you can decide whether or not to return to your safe, noncompetitive, unselfish world."

Her eyes widened and her plush lips parted, but he forged on. "I won't take anything from you that you're not willing to give, Ash."

Her eyes slid closed and she let out a soft, mournful groan, but her body swayed against him. "I don't know how much I can give."

"You'll know, Ash. You'll know." He stroked her lips again until she parted them. "Life is so temporary, sweetheart. This will be just for us. For right now."

Her breath warm and moist against the pad of his thumb, she whispered, "What if I want more than right now?"

A spark of hope flared only to be ruthlessly squelched. Knowing she wouldn't want more the moment she learned the truth about who he was and why he'd come to Plainview, he stroked her lip, coaxing little kisses from her.

He assured her, "Then you'll have more." The lie burned the back of his throat, but he pressed on. "Either way, it'll be okay, because whatever happens tomorrow, or the next day, won't change what we'll have had tonight."

Her eyes stayed closed, but she raised her other

hand to his hip, and Mac waited for her to either push him away or urge him closer to the undeniable force that was already pulling him into her.

She did neither. Instead she drew in a deep breath that raised her breasts against his chest and asked, "Is there someone special in your life, Mac, someone you've made plans with, commitments to, back in New York?"

While he sure as hell hadn't made any commitments to Stephanie, he had made one to Kate, though she'd never had the chance to live in New York.

When he hesitated, she opened her eyes and met his. The wanting in her gaze nearly took him out at the knees.

He couldn't deny her. They could have this short time together. They could. "No, Ash. There's no one back home."

Only in his heart.

Ghosts of pain and betrayal flared in her eyes. "How do I know I can trust you? How do I know you're not just after my family's money?"

He suppressed a snort. That was usually his line. "I've never made a secret of what I want from you."

"What *exactly* is that, Mac?"

He didn't dare look that closely at his wants where this woman was concerned. They didn't matter, anyway.

He bent and feathered a kiss to a corner of her mouth, savoring her swift intake of air. "To be with you tonight. Maybe tomorrow night, too. Hell, we can throw in everything in between."

"But you're not asking for a one-night stand."

"You're over thinking this, Ash. Let your body decide. Give yourself permission to just be. Worry about tomorrow when it comes."

Everything would end after she saw the caption beneath the picture he was certain would be on the society page in the Sunday paper. And though it wouldn't be a car accident putting a painful end to all the possibilities, he was still just as responsible.

Chapter Eight

Ashley went up on her toes and put her mouth to his with such sweet purpose that Mac exploded in so many tiny, bright lights the astronomers would forever wonder what in the hell happened over the Rivers estate.

He kissed her back for all he was worth, gathering her in his arms to help buffer her from the storm of his own need, halfway afraid of what he might be unleashing on her. They kissed deep and hard, like they had after she'd knocked him down into the gully, but this time the knowledge of what would come next made the contact that much hotter. Like before, the need to cover her with his body hit him with the force of a rogue wave off Oahu's north shore.

He pulled his lips from hers and bent to scoop her off her feet.

She made a funny noise, a sort of whispered squawk.

He teased, "What? Now that we're doing something naughty, you think you have to be quiet?"

"I would rather not wake up Grandmother, Donavon, or Marie," she whispered.

"Yeah. And bouncing a basketball is so much quieter. Trust me, if no one has come to see what's going on down here by now, no one's coming." He turned and carried her to the break in the hedge.

"You're not seriously going to carry me into the house and up the stairs, are you?"

"Of course I am. I wouldn't miss this chance to show off what a manly man I am for you." He grinned to ease the worry that lingered deep in her eyes and in the lines on either side of her pretty mouth. "Me Mac. You Ash Bash."

It worked. She smiled and relaxed her head against his shoulder. "I can think of much better ways to show off your manliness, Mac," she purred and ran a hand up the back of his neck into his hair. He shuddered in pleasure. "And actually, I think that chaise lounge right there would be the perfect place to do it."

He stopped, looking from the lounge chair with its overstuffed pad to her, unable to hide his surprise. He'd figured her for the lights out, only under the covers sort. Though after what he'd learned about her tonight, he needed to reevaluate all of his presumptions about Miss Ashley Rivers.

Deep down he feared this new Ashley would be harder to resist, harder to walk away from. He pushed the thought aside. That was the last thing he wanted to think about right now.

She shrugged and linked her hands on the side of his neck to pull herself up far enough in his arms to nuzzle his ear. "Hey, if I'm finally going to start living, I might as well give it a good start," she whispered. "I've often lain here by the pool, imagining opening my arms to a gorgeous hunk of a man illuminated by starlight from above, candlelight from below..."

He chuckled. "Look out, world, the rich girl's going wild."

"With her very own Wild Man," she murmured in his ear, then touched her hot little tongue to the outer whorl.

Every nerve ending in his body responded with a big *oh yeah*. But he didn't want her to have any regrets about what happened between them in the next few hours. "As much as I want to make more than a few of your fantasies come true tonight, sunshine, I have a need to get you in my bed. Will that work for you?"

She sighed into his ear, making him shiver in delicious agony again. "If you insist."

"I do. Because I want to see your gorgeous hair fanned out on my pillow. I want to see the sheets bunched in your fists. I want to—"

"Enough, already. Get me there. Oh, wait." She squirmed in his arms until he had no choice but to let her legs drop and set her on her feet.

Afraid she had changed her mind or thought of some repressive reason why they couldn't make love, he couldn't bring himself to release her entirely. "What?"

"I have to do something first." She smiled sensually, reassuring him only enough to let her back out of his embrace.

Frowning his suspicion, he asked, "What?"

She used the toe of the opposite foot to pull one of her shoes off, then the other, and said, "This." With one big step to the side, she jumped into the shallow end of the pool. Water sluiced around her, soaking her to the neck.

Mac stared in openmouthed delight. "Oh, my—"

"I was all stinky and sweaty."

"Yeah, but I liked that."

"Well, I didn't." She moved to the edge of the pool. "Though now that I'm in here, I realize that chlorine isn't much better."

He bent and offered her a hand. "I'll get over it."

She reached up and grabbed his hand with both of hers. "Especially after *this*." She yanked on him, pulling him headfirst into the pool.

Coming up sputtering and laughing and way too happy with this wild side of Ashley, Mac wiped the hair and water back away from his face.

Her smile was sweet and sexy as hell. "Now we both smell like chlorine."

After retrieving his floating soccer slides and setting them on the pool's edge, he glided to her and caught her up around the waist, bringing her body tight against his arousal. He could feel every luscious inch of her through their wet clothes. "But what do we taste like?"

Her gaze dropped to his mouth, her expression sobering with obvious anticipation as she wrapped her arms around his neck. "I guess we'll have to find out."

Their lips met, tasting, licking, probing. She did taste a little of chlorine, thanks to his dunking, but mostly she tasted of hot, sexy woman. He backed her against the side of the pool and brought one of her legs up to his hip. Cupping a full breast in his hand, he ground himself against her and deepened their kiss, amazed the pool water didn't start to boil. His world narrowed to her hot mouth, taut nipples, and perfect grooves. He had never wanted to make love to a woman more in his life.

He slid his hand from her breast and reached down between them to pull her shorts aside, to find and stroke what he couldn't wait to get to and make her as hot for him as he was for her, but Ashley pulled away from his kiss.

"Mac, if we're going to make it up to that bed you talked about, we better go now."

He didn't need to be told twice. He gripped her beneath the arms and hoisted her out of the pool, setting her on her bottom on the edge. She swung her legs up and out, then stood as he climbed from the pool. He shook himself like a dog as she used his towel to get as much of the water as she could out of her tank top and shorts.

Tossing him the towel, she peeled off her wet socks and wrung them out while he dried off his soaked T-shirt and swim trunks. She stuffed the socks in her shoes and hurried for the door to the house. Mac didn't want her out of his contact for that long, so he slung the towel over his shoulder, slipped his feet into his slides and hustled to catch her. He snatched her back up into his arms to carry her again.

"Mac," she protested softly, but wrapped her arms helpfully around his neck, her running shoes poking him in the ear.

Pausing only long enough for her to enter the code

into the security system after they went through the door, Mac carried her up to his room feeling indeed like a manly man with a beautiful princess in his arms.

A princess in soaking wet basketball gear with the power to rock his world, yanking loose all the pitons that had held him fast all these years.

He didn't care. He decided to buy into his line about living life, about not over thinking the situation.

He let his body decide.

Despite her protests about her wet clothes, he laid her carefully on the big, moonlight-washed, four-poster bed, its brown and navy striped bedding—also chosen to appeal to male guests—already rumpled from his earlier attempt to sleep. With Ashley draped across it, her lids half-closed and her lips moistened in anticipation, the bedding was more than appealing.

"Holy haggis," he groaned more to himself than her.

She smiled tremulously and lifted a hand toward him.

Saints help him for thinking he could make love with her and survive unscathed. But he was nothing if not scarred.

He peeled off his wet shirt and lay down next to her. He ran a hand beneath her jersey. Her skin was hot and damp, the muscles in her stomach firm and strong. She pulled his mouth to hers just as his hand reached the curve of her breast, and her tongue met his the same instant her nipple peaked against his palm through her wet, lacy and definitely nonsports bra.

They both moaned.

He was supposed to be showing her what she'd

been missing, but Mac feared he was about to get a hell of a lesson. He hadn't exactly lived the life of a monk the past decade, but he hadn't cared about why the ladies in question needed the release they'd found with him. The same wasn't true with Ashley.

A moment of very unmanly panic gripped him. He'd made a vow to Kate.

He yanked his mouth from Ashley's and rolled away.

She rolled with him, covering him the way he'd imagined covering her. She kissed the underside of his jaw, the top of his chin, then murmured against his lips as she tilted her pelvis against him, "I can't believe what you do to me, Mac."

The air left his lungs in a rush. He realized he'd opened the floodgates, so he had no choice but to ride the wave. Too bad he knew damn well he wanted this even more than she did. With Ashley in his arms, for the first time in a decade the throbbing ache of losing Kate ebbed away, replaced by a surge of wanting.

She kissed him hard again and he stopped thinking.

He pulled the clinging, wet basketball jersey up and broke the kiss long enough to get it over her head. Then he connected with her again. But it wasn't enough, and he could tell she knew it, too. She unfastened her bra and allowed him to fill his hands with her lush breasts and his brain with unbearable need.

He rolled her on her back, but held up a hand to stop her from reaching for his black swim trunks. "Wait a second. Don't move."

He ducked into the bathroom and tore through his shaving kit, looking for the smashed package of condoms he remembered seeing in there. He'd meant it when he'd said this wouldn't cost her.

Little blue package in hand, he returned to the side of the bed. She'd moved, but only to free her hair from the elastic band that had held it and spread it out in a golden halo on the bed. She was so beautiful...she really was going to kill him. He shucked his swim trunks and peeled her mesh shorts and panties from her hips, pausing long enough to kiss the red indentations made by the short's elastic waistband on her delicate stomach. She giggled and squirmed beneath his lips. He burned with satisfaction.

And he was more than ready. But he wanted to do this right, to give her something worthwhile to remember. She deserved so much more, but this was all he had to give. Guilt hovered over his shoulders, but he swatted it away before it found a place to settle. He *would* have this night with her.

He worked his way farther down her sleek belly, pausing where he knew she expected him to go, but continuing downward, filling his head with the scent chlorine could never mask from the animal in him.

Ever since she'd trotted from the house in her skimpy running shorts he'd been obsessing about her sculpted runner thighs. He settled himself between her legs and slipped one hand beneath her right thigh.

She flexed automatically—almost a flinch. He reassured her by placing a soft kiss on her smooth inner thigh. Her legs were so long, so strong, but elegant. So inexplicably Ashley.

He licked along the contour of her muscle until she squirmed again.

She half moaned, half laughed. "Mac, you're tickling me."

Lifting his head, he said, "You have the best legs."

She raised a hand toward him and rasped, "Then come up here and get on with it so I can wrap them around you."

He grinned, hot need pumping through him. "Now that's what I call a proper invitation."

After donning the condom, he settled his body on top of hers and tried to focus past the roar of his heartbeat in his ears. He wanted to kiss her, touch her, make her writhe with wanting before he buried himself in her.

She had other plans.

It took her all of two seconds to spread her legs, settle him against her, then tilt her pelvis and push upward. He was deep inside of her, held tight and set on fire by her heat, before he had time to draw a breath.

"Holy haggis, Ashley, don't move." He wouldn't be much of a studly type if she finished him off with one motion.

"I have to, Mac," she pleaded, burying her face beneath his chin.

"I know, but man, you feel so…"

Then they were both moving, crashing through the world on the avalanche their needs had broken free.

Though they weren't out on the chaise lounge next to the pool, together they added a few more stars to the night sky, and Mac knew in his gut he'd never be able to look up at night without remembering.

ASHLEY SETTLED HER CHEEK more comfortably on the solid swell of Mac's biceps and stared out the window at the few stars bright enough to compete with the moon's glow. He murmured something incomprehensible and smoothed the hair on the back of her head away from his face, then settled his hand possessively on her sheet-covered hip. While a particular firmness against her backside made it clear he wasn't entirely sated, he seemed content to just hold her spoon-fashion for a time.

She still wasn't certain if she'd made the right choice listening to his logic—not to mention her own heart and desires—but she had never felt anything so wonderful in her life. Mac's kisses, his touch, had opened the door to a powerful need that never would have been satisfied by her family's well-managed life, no matter how good the paté.

His exhilarating pursuit, and capture, of her felt like an entry drug to life. The life she'd willingly forfeited to avoid another disaster like Roger. But out on the basketball court she'd decided to take the chance because Mac was so different from Roger.

Mac walked through the house without so much as a glance at Grandmother's costly art collection or the valuable antiques. He never asked her about the important people she might know and when he could meet them. Just the opposite. She'd had to pull him around the room at the banquet, and it had been filled to the brim with people who could do a lot for him, both occupationally and socially. Mac only seemed to care about the reasons behind the choices she'd made, the wants she'd denied.

He'd asked her questions she'd been too afraid to ask herself, and he made her feel like he cared about her answers. Though it wasn't easy to justify what she'd done—and hadn't done—in her life, his concern filled up so many of the holes worn into her soul by her uncertainties.

In retrospect, it was clear that Roger had only been interested in what her family had, in what their lifestyle represented. From the beginning Mac had only been interested in one thing—challenging her in one way or another.

And she liked it.

She liked how he made her feel. She liked how he could give her a thrill with nothing more than a look. And she especially liked how alive he made her feel, as if her true self was breaking out of the restrictive cocoon she'd been wrapped in for so long.

For the first time in her life she was going to worry about tomorrow when it came. Tonight she wanted to be with Mac in the place only he'd been able to take her to—a place where she could be herself.

A place where she could trust.

When he apparently sensed she wasn't sleeping, he moved her hair out of the way and started kissing her neck and teasing his hardness against her backside, obviously willing to take her to that place again.

Ashley arched her back to accept his invitation. The rough texture of his palm felt so good as he ran his hand over her belly and upward to cup her breast. She never wanted the feeling to end.

This time their lovemaking was slow and sensual, with him seeming to make a point of touching every inch of her until she felt she was floating in a mist of sensation. She never wanted to leave where only he could take her.

Fortunately for her, he was willing to take her there yet again right before dawn.

And she loved it.

MAC WATCHED ASHLEY'S HAIR turn into liquid sunshine as she bent to don her shorts, the light streaming through the window behind her sending her into an endearing panic. While he understood her desire to not be caught coming out of his room by her grandmother or any of the household staff, he wasn't done with her yet.

Especially considering the way his body reacted to the sight of her sliding her shorts up her long, toned legs. He'd missed her putting on her bra and tank top, having been sound asleep when she first slipped out of bed. He realized there were a few spots on her gorgeous body he'd yet to explore.

Clearing the sleep from his throat but helpless against the hunger in his tone, he said, "Those clothes have got to be damp still. Why don't you take them off and let them dry some more. I'm sure we could think of something to do while you wait."

She glanced up from looking for her socks. Her pupils flared in recognition of what his *something* would entail and she smiled shyly before retrieving her socks and shoes from where she'd tossed them. "It's getting late."

He shrugged a bare shoulder. "Yeah, so? What do you have to do today?"

"Well, it's Saturday, so I need to—"

"Sleep in late? Well, not actually sleep..."

"No, I have to—"

"Take the day off."

She paused pulling an obviously wet sock right side out. "But—"

"Spend the day with me." He wasn't ready for their time together to end. He wanted to cheat fate out of as much happiness as he could. He wanted to be with her.

"Doing what?" she asked.

He waggled his brows and patted the bed next to him, the sheet hanging on to the warmth left behind by her body like an equally ardent lover.

She laughed, then shook her head at him. "How about if *you* spend the day with *me?*" she challenged.

"Doing what?" he echoed her question.

She smiled sweetly but the spark of the devil lit her eyes. "Attending a luncheon for this year's recipients of the Rivers Foundation scholarships."

He seriously considered her offer for a moment, but figured he'd face the same perils as he had at the banquet the night before. Her finding out the truth in the newspaper was going to be bad enough. He shook his head. "I wouldn't be able to keep my hands off you. Not after last night."

"And this morning."

"And this morning," he agreed, trumping her sexy smile with one of his own. Deciding he wasn't going to let her escape him just yet, he eased himself toward the edge of the bed.

Her gaze darted to where the sheet had fallen away

from his hips and her jaw dropped. "Again? Oh, no, you don't, Mac." She wadded her wet socks in her fist, shoved her feet into her running shoes and made for the door to the rest of his bedroom suite. "It's late enough as it is. I truly have to go."

"Ashley." The seriousness of his tone stopped her. "Find me as soon as you get home."

She met his gaze with a tenderness and genuine pleasure in her sea-blue eyes that made mincemeat of his iron hide. "I will."

And then she was gone, and he fell back on his pillow, for the first time in a decade cursing the fact that a MacDougal only loved once.

HER WATCH READ TEN TO SIX by the time Ashley arrived back home that evening, and as much as she wanted to race through the house looking for Mac, she headed for the main staircase. She needed to take to her rooms the one item too precious to entrust to a delivery service.

She tucked her day planner against her body to glide a reverent hand down the tiny garment bag draped over her arm. The christening gown had come through the cleaning process intact, thank heavens. She would have been devastated if anything had happened to the tiny, white silk and lace gown that had seen Harrison and herself, and their father before them, christened.

Nathan would wear the gown next, though it would be a tight fit, not the loose, flowing one intended. Harrison's sweet little boy had been late coming into their lives.

At least he'd come. Nathan—and his mother, too—had brought a lot of joy into this house.

Ashley held the gown steady on her arm as she mounted the stairs, her chest constricting tight around her heart. Would she be able to bring that kind of joy into her life with a baby of her own? Before last night, she would have quickly answered no. Now she wasn't so sure. A baby with Mac—

She stopped herself from finishing the thought. She was jumping the proverbial shotgun. Figuring out if she could have a future with Mac needed to come first. And she wanted to figure it out. He had made her want things, things she'd given up hoping for, from the moment she laid eyes on him.

The need to lay eyes, not to mention other parts, on him immediately seized her with tingling urgency. She hurried to her rooms, halfway hoping to find him waiting for her there, especially when she caught a whiff of his spicy scent in her office. But when she found her bedroom empty, the disappointment that swamped her was stunning. Straightening her spine against the intensity of the emotion, she went to hang the christening gown in her closet.

While he'd seemed to enjoy being in bed with her, Mac wasn't the type to laze around waiting for her to join him, and he certainly wouldn't have risked being caught in a compromising position. He'd been thus far accommodating to her need for secrecy, which she greatly appreciated. She'd have to remember to thank him for it.

Leaving her room, a piece of her stationery tented on her desk caught her eye. She went to the desk and picked it up. A strong, clear handwriting covered the page.

Meet me down by the river. Wear something comfortable—and easy to take off.

Ashley's body knew without a signature who the letter was from. Her heart pounded and her cheeks flushed with expectant heat. She kicked off her pumps and ran for her closet, stripping her white linen suit as she went. In less than five minutes she'd changed into a soft pair of jeans she'd purchased to play with Nathan in and a sky-blue cashmere sweater with a deep V neckline she hoped would appeal to Mac. Leather sandals she could easily slip off went on last.

After brushing her hair out of its French twist, she hurried from her bedroom, automatically picking up her day planner as she passed her desk. Mac's voice sounded in her head.

No. You don't need it. Not today.

And she didn't. She set it back down. The only thing she needed today was the feeling Mac gave her. The feeling that she was wanted and appreciated for the woman she was deep down inside.

She picked up his invitation instead, a giddy excitement bubbling through her, and headed for the river.

She actually ran down the fine gravel path leading from the veranda, past the oak tree, and on toward a hedge break, until moisture-laden air hit her when she reached the crest where the manicured lawn sloped down to the edge of the gently flowing McKenzie River. At the end of the little dock jutting into the water she spotted Mac stretched out on his side, ankles crossed, on a red, white, and gray-checked wool stadium blanket with a large, covered wicker basket next to him.

He had on a faded blue baseball hat, his standard snug, white T-shirt, well-worn jeans, and scuffed, brown cowboy boots. The bill of his cap and the tilt of his head shielded his face from her as well as the bright spring sun, but she couldn't mistake the thick, sun-streaked brown hair curling up around the edge of the hat. Or the width of the shoulders ridged with muscles as he supported himself on one elbow and watched the dark-green waters of the river slip by.

What looked like a picnic feast was already spread out on the blanket, complete with tall, brass candlesticks and slender white candles. A spurt of tenderness and appreciation blurred her vision. The man had already seduced her body, now he was seducing her heart.

Ashley feared he'd already won it.

Mac's dark head turned toward her and he waved her down. "You better hurry over here before some other babe steals your spot, sunshine!"

Laughter rose in her, forcing the fear and uncertainty Roger had branded her with far from her consciousness. She started toward Mac, her step light and confident. "I'm not worried. I've a mean elbow, you know!" she called back, waggling said body part at him.

He laughed, too, the rich sound rising on the evening breeze along with the moist scent of the river. "Boy, do you ever."

When she reached the dock, his hot, golden-brown gaze made her too warm in her sweater. She should have known she'd be impervious to the crispness of the evening air with Mac around. Pausing at the edge of the blanket, she surveyed the plates of finger food—crackers heaped with smoked salmon spread, chunks of brie cheese topped with red and green grapes, and chocolate-dipped strawberries.

Impressed, she commented, "You went to an awful lot of trouble, Mr. Wild. Would I be wrong in assuming you have an end result in mind?"

He chuckled as he indicated for her to have a seat on the blanket next to him. "And here I thought my note would be the tip-off."

She slipped off her sandals and sat down, giving him a salacious grin of her own. "You were already guaranteed that, Mac."

He shoved back the bill of his hat and slapped his forehead. "Now you tell me." He reached for an uncorked bottle of red wine and poured them each a glass. "But I figured you could use a little R and R after a day in the fund-raising jungle." He put the bottle down and handed her a glass.

"You figured right." Her fingers lingered over his on the stem of the crystal goblet. His skin felt so familiar, their connection so natural. The wine glowed like a rare jewel in the light of the low-slung sun. His eyes glowed like a man certain of an evening's outcome.

Her pulse thundered with the same certainty. She took a sip of the wine without breaking eye contact.

A wicked brow twitched.

But she wanted to savor this evening the same way she savored the heady taste of the wine on her tongue.

She wanted to make it last forever. She settled herself more comfortably on the thick blanket, crossing her outstretched legs at the ankle and leaning on one elbow as he had. "After spending the day with a bunch of women, I could also use a little masculine conversation. Tell me about your business, Mac."

He fiddled with his glass for a moment, then reached for a cracker and popped it in his mouth. Finally he said, "I do all right for myself. And I enjoy what I do. I really like that I don't have to be stuck in an office all the time, that I can do my job while in the great outdoors." He waved an expansive hand at the river.

The thought that he would be in great demand in the ecologically sensitive Pacific Northwest made her palms damp. Did she dare ask him to stay after he finished helping her brother out? She settled for a more general comment. "There's a lot of demand for specialists like you around here. Though I'm sure you're used to being a popular guy."

He shrugged and reached for another cracker. His self-deprecating smile endeared him even more to her. "There are plenty out there not happy to see me."

"Polluters mostly, I'd imagine."

He shrugged again.

She cocked her head at him, wondering at his evasiveness. Was he ashamed of his life? Did he think she wouldn't value him because he didn't wear a designer suit or sport a golden parachute?

Wanting to connect with him the same way he'd connected with her on the basketball court, to be someone he could trust with his secrets like she'd trusted him, she pressed, "What about your family, Mac? Tell me about them. Where do they live?"

He took a rather long drink of wine. "My family's all in New York City, or there about. That's where I grew up."

She extended a foot and nudged his scuffed boots. "Urban cowboy?"

"Aren't they all?"

She sputtered on a sip of wine.

While she recovered, he continued, "My folks live, er, in a place that they share with most of my brothers and sisters."

"Brothers and sisters? Wow. I have to say I'm surprised to hear you have siblings. I've always thought of you as the lone wolf type."

He smirked. "Well, they *are* there and I *am* here."

"How many of each?"

"I have two brothers and two sisters. All younger than me."

"My goodness. Are they all as attractive as you?"

He met her gaze, his expression shifting to the predatory gleam she realized she had grown most used to. "So you find me attractive, Miss Ashley?"

She cocked a brow of her own and allowed all of her attraction toward him to show in her eyes. "You have no idea, Mr. Wild."

He made a growling sound deep in his throat and leaned toward her. "Comments like that will never get you through dessert, sunshine."

"Better for my waistline that way."

He grunted in response and pushed himself up off

his elbow. With slow purpose, he turned his baseball cap around so the bill wouldn't be in the way.

The simple sureness of the act turned her on. She wetted her lips in anticipation.

Bracing himself with one hand, he reached for her with his other. He slipped his fingers into her hair and drew her toward him, leaning forward himself until their lips met. His kiss held the memory of their lovemaking along with the promise of more to come.

Ashley moaned deep in her throat, loving the way he made her feel, the freedom he offered her true self.

Mac broke off the kiss and leaned back, his fingertips tracing a sensual retreat along her jaw. "Damn, I wish it got a lot darker a lot quicker this time of year."

Her brain fogged with desire, she asked stupidly, "Why?"

He reached back up and cupped her cheek with such tenderness her heart soared. "Because I want to make love to you right here, right now, but tonight I'd planned on giving you that candlelight and starlight you wanted."

She nuzzled his palm, planting kisses on its warm strength and said the words she'd been thinking all day. "Interesting enough, it turns out all I really want is a regular guy, used to living a regular life—" she flicked her gaze to his well-loved looking baseball hat "—in regular clothes."

Right or wrong, good or bad, Ashley jumped into love with Mac Wild with both feet. "And I want him for more than just a couple of nights."

Chapter Nine

Ashley stopped kissing Mac's palm when she realized he'd frozen. Dread trickled into her stomach. She'd said too much too soon. He'd been talking her into a casual relationship out there on the basketball court, one with no expectations. Yet she hadn't made it twenty-four hours without asking for more.

She met his gaze, looking for the horror, the rejection. What she thought she saw was understanding, and perhaps…sadness? She knew she'd seen that look in his eyes before. When they'd been with Harrison, Juliet and Nathan in the kitchen, speaking of family.

He closed his eyes and kissed her before she could be sure what emotion lay beneath his soulful look. His kiss was overwhelmingly sweet and poignant and touched her so deeply she feared she'd weep. But she didn't want to cry and risk driving him further into this strange, melancholy place he seemed to be.

She didn't want him feeling that way because of her. She didn't want to ruin the wonderful evening he'd created. And after surviving the fire of last night without burning to a crisp, she didn't particularly want sweet and poignant right now.

He wanted Ash Bash, so she'd give him Ash Bash.

She broke off the kiss and sent him what she hoped to be a saucy grin. "And maybe I'll meet that regular guy before I'm too old to know what to do with him." Then she snatched his hat from his head, scrambled to her feet, and took off running up the dock toward the lawn.

She glanced over her shoulder to see if Mac had caught on to her game, but he was just staring after her with lowered brows and a slightly gaping mouth, his hair an odd mixture of hat-head and wild disarray.

She stopped and dangled his hat over the water. "Come on, Mac! I bet you can't catch a wild rich girl!"

His mouth curled into a confident, decidedly wicked smile as he pushed himself to his feet with the powerful grace of a cougar on the hunt. "And here I thought you weren't going to make bets with me anymore."

She started backing up, her heart pounding from the thrill, and no small measure of delicious fear, of being his chosen prey. She hadn't felt this alive in years. "I changed my mind."

"Ah," he said, loose-limbed and casual. He took a few steps, then exploded into motion, his boots loud on the wood, his long, powerful legs closing the distance between them so fast she squeaked and bailed off the dock onto the grassy bank, barely missing the water.

She ran a few steps, her toes digging into the cool, thick grass and releasing the pungent smell of the river mud. Feeling him draw near, she made a quick change of direction and darted up the slope toward drier land. She laughed when she felt his hand graze her waist as he missed getting a hold of her. She tried one more directional change, but he'd anticipated her move and snaked a strong, tan arm around her middle.

With a triumphant "Gotcha!" he captured her against his hard chest then dragged her to the soft grass.

She squealed with laughter, loving the play, and the way it made her feel so alive. He rolled her to her back, her hair a crazy tangle over her face, and trapped her between his arms while he held himself above her. His heat sought her out of its own accord, a sharp contrast to the cool earth beneath her. She surrendered to the urge to arch into him.

His smile was wide and gorgeous and a prime example of masculine satisfaction. "Looks like I just caught myself a wild rich girl."

Wanting to shout with happiness, she pushed her hair off her face, meeting his smiling, topaz gaze. "And it looks like I just found myself a regular guy in the guise of a wild man."

His smile faded and the gleam left his eyes. Ashley's stomach clenched in response to the sinking sensation of dread. She feared she'd made another grave error. He clearly didn't want to be *her guy*. He would then be unable to characterize what was happening between them as casual.

He had to know there was more to what was happening between them than a meaningless fling. It was in his kiss. It was in the way he went ahead and lowered his body half on her and half on his side. He had to know what was developing between them, he just apparently didn't want to admit it. Acknowledging what they had would go against his afore-sworn beliefs.

But beliefs could change. Especially with the right enticements.

She hitched one leg over his and sighed with joy at the contact. Tangling herself up with Mac felt so right that the specter of her past mistake faded away. It had never felt this right with Roger. Actually she'd never felt much of anything with Roger.

The admission embarrassed her. She'd come so close to picking him to spend her life with. A life that would have ultimately been filled with betrayal.

Compared to what she was experiencing with Mac, it would have been a very sad life, indeed.

Mac raised a hand and brushed her hair farther back from her face, his fingers gliding with heavenly gentleness against her scalp. His gaze following the path of his fingers, he murmured, "Oh, Ash Bash. What am I going to do with you?"

His confusion scared her. She didn't want him thinking he had to *do* something with her, that he had to make a decision now. Not tonight. She *did* want to be Ash Bash tonight.

To distract him she offered, "Kissing would be good. At least to start." Memories of their lovemaking flooded her mind with images that made her body tighten and burn with need. "Then that second thing you did last night would be nice."

He chuckled and she felt the vibrations of his chest against hers. "That second thing—oh, yeah. You mean when I took your leg and hitched it up like this?" He slipped his arm behind the knee she'd draped over him and brought her leg up until he held it in the crook of his elbow, angling his own leg between hers.

Ashley sucked in the brisk, river-damp air between her teeth at the sensations sparking from the contact. "That would be the one. Now, for the kissing part." She reached up and buried her hand in his thick hair, loving the feel of it between her fingers.

Already in the process of lowering his head, he accepted her kiss with the sort of ready passion she expected from him, rather than the poignant, sweet kiss of earlier. He must have realized she wasn't going to press him or try to force him into a commitment. At least not right now.

It was the honesty of his wanting that made her sure she was making the right choice, that taking this chance wasn't a mistake.

He inched her leg higher with an increase of the pressure from his flexed thigh, and Ashley stopped thinking about anything except the way Mac's hot, solid body felt against her. And the way he made her ache for him deep inside.

Without breaking their kiss, he pushed her sweater up, his big, callused hand, not the crisp evening air, responsible for the shiver racing across her skin. She slid her hands down his sides until she found the hem of his T-shirt, then worked her way beneath in search of his hot skin. She alternated gliding her fingers over the smooth flesh of his chest and back and clutching his hard muscles, depending on what he was doing to her. The need throbbing low in her pelvis escalated until it reverberated in her soul.

He seemed to hear it and answered the call by unfastening her jeans and slipping his hand beneath the lacy top of her panties. He worked his hand down far enough that he could touch her where she most wanted to be touched.

He stroked her until she was ready to climb his frame, then made it worse—or was it better?—by dipping his fingers deeper. Ashley clung to his shoulders and sought to anchor herself to his mouth, determined not to let the storm crest over her yet. Just when she feared she was about to lose the battle against the impending climax, he slipped his hand back up to her belly, then beneath her sweater to tease her breast again.

They kissed and touched until they were both panting and literally steaming in the cool air.

Mac pulled away, scrubbing a hand over his face. "Listen, as intent as I am on making all your fantasies come true, a woman like you, who's used to the finer things in life, deserves a bed."

Ashley blinked and looked hard at him through the deepening twilight. Did he think she had to have everything first class? Was that what made him seem melancholy? That he couldn't afford to provide her with the things he thought she required? "What do you mean, a woman like me?"

He lowered his head and met her gaze, his eyes amber in the dim light, but still warm and guileless. "The kind who deserves to be held all night long."

Ashamed by her need for reassurance, she cupped

his square jaw in her hands, his emerging beard scratchy against her palms. "Just held?"

He grinned, his straight white teeth brighter than usual in the approaching dark. "I'll do whatever you ask, sunshine."

"Will you stay?" The words were out before Ashley could stop herself. So much for not pressing. But she couldn't help it. She wanted this to last. For how long, she didn't dare speculate. She only knew a month was not long enough.

Mac's smile faded again, his expression foreboding. Just when Ashley was about to say that she meant only that he stay through the night, he dropped his forehead to hers and rubbed noses with her. "Ask me again tomorrow, Ash. By then you might change your mind."

The ominous feeling of dread she'd experienced earlier bubbled like a fountain from her stomach into her chest. "Why, Mac? Why would I change my mind?"

He planted a kiss on the end of her nose and leveraged himself upward. "Because a man can only perform like a god for so long, sunshine. I'm bound to disappoint you in the sack eventually. Especially if you keep getting me so damn hot so damn fast."

The dread sluiced out of her with the force of a river breaching a collapsed dike. Almost dizzy with relief that he'd been thinking about the sex, not his unwillingness to commit, she reached up, grabbed him by the hair, and yanked him down for a long, molten kiss. She found his tongue with hers, stroking with the same sensual purpose he used on her to make his point. She wanted him to have no doubt that she felt the same fire, the same driving need.

When she finally let him up for air, she grinned a seductive, heavy-lidded smile. "Don't worry, big guy. I'm sure I can find a way to keep up with you."

He groaned and rolled away from her, taking his heat with him. Ashley shivered, the contrast between his embrace and the touch of the night air painful.

Sitting up, he said, "In that case, we'd better stop in the kitchen on our way upstairs to stock up on liquids. I have a feeling I'm going to need it to keep from shriveling up into nothing." He stood and offered her his hand.

"Poor baby. I can think of worse ways to go."

He closed his eyes for a moment, then turned his face toward the darkening horizon. "So can I, Ash. So can I."

His solemn tone gave her pause. But trusting him in a way she'd never trusted a man before, she slipped her hand into his, gaining as much bliss from the warm, sure, gentle strength of his grip as he pulled her to her feet as she did from his lovemaking.

And when he pulled her into his embrace, squeezing her tightly to him, Ashley rejoiced. She wouldn't have to live out her life alone, aching for what she'd thought she couldn't have because of her determination to protect her family from unscrupulous fortune hunters and liars. She could have love and keep her father's approval.

With Mac, she could have it all: the confidence that her family was safe and well cared for, and a man to share her life with, to have children with.

Mac held Ashley close, waiting for the crippling waves of grief, regret, and the worst of them all, guilt, to wash over him when her words about ways to go had reminded him of Kate's death. But they never came. All he felt was the beating of Ashley's heart at the base of his rib cage. The heat of their perfect physical connection. The grounding trust in her embrace.

A trust he didn't deserve.

So the guilt came after all. But it wasn't guilt over choosing his own wants and needs over Kate's wishes. He felt guilty for lying to the woman who might have the power to heal him.

A woman he'd never be able to love.

He wasn't free to commit to her the way she deserved.

But he could give them both some incredible memories, memories that would get him through the lifetime of long, lonely nights that lay ahead of him like an endless, desolate road. So he released her from his embrace and took her hand, leading her back to the dock.

Noticing her raised eyebrows, he said, "Since we have to stop in the kitchen anyway, we might as well drop this stuff off there." He gestured at the picnic spread.

"Ah. For a moment, I thought that you'd changed your mind about the whole bed thing."

"Well..." He tapped a finger against his chin as he considered the blanket for a moment, mentally weighing its thickness against the hard-looking dock planking. Then he looked up at the stars emerging in the early-night sky. "It's grown darker a lot faster than I thought it would. I suppose if you were on top, only your knees would suffer..."

Ashley laughed, the sound deep and hearty and carried by the river's breath like a siren's song. "Sore knees are a small price to pay for a fantasy come true, Mac." She dropped to said knees and cleared the blanket of their picnic with a crashing, clattering sweep of an arm. "There," she said with startling satisfaction and met his shocked look with a pleased grin.

"I would have never thought you capable of such willful destruction, Miss Ashley."

"It seems you bring out only the best in me, Mr. Wild. Now come here. I don't want to wait a second longer to have you inside of me."

"Lord, woman, when you put it that way..." Mac dropped down next to Ashley and reached for her, but she knocked him flat on his back and straddled him, surprising a belly laugh out of him.

She squirmed and bounced until he was about ready to flip her on her back and get on with it. She finally stilled and pronounced, "The knees will survive."

"But I won't if you don't let me kiss you."

She giggled and let him pull her down until their lips met. He filled his mouth, his hands, his senses with her to the point where he thought he'd explode. Grabbing the edge of the big blanket, he rolled her off of him and onto her side and covered them both up in one motion. As she wiggled out of her jeans, he pushed his out of the way, donned his protection, then shoved both their shirts up so he could do the third thing that he'd done to her the night before.

He rubbed his chest against hers, ticking the tips of

her breasts with the hair on his chest, then moving lower to repeat the process with his mouth. Sliding lower still, he worshiped her beautiful body, her delicate scent imprinting on his brain, until she grabbed him by the hair and pulled him up. He kissed his way back to her mouth, then slid inside her like a thief into heaven.

It was even better than it had been the first time, and Mac cursed himself for a fool.

THE NIGHT WENT TOO FAST.

Mac had wanted to draw out his time with Ashley, cramming as many memories as he could into the hours between dusk down by the river and the breaking dawn he intended to watch with her. But as soon as the heated flush of fulfillment started to wear off, he noticed Ashley shivering despite the blanket pulled beneath her chin and the fact that she lay tight against his side with her head resting on his shoulder.

He wrapped his arms around her and held her closer. "Are you cold?"

He felt her chin move up and down on his chest. "The temperature has dropped quite a bit."

"I guess staying out here until dawn is not an option. You about done resoluting?"

She lifted her head from his shoulder to look at him, her hair standing out every which way in the best-looking mess he'd ever seen. "Excuse me?"

"Boy, you really don't get out. Resoluting. You know, coming down after—"

"I get the picture." She laughed, then shivered again. "Brrr. Yes, I guess I'm done *resoluting*." She slid a hand across his chest to wrap her arm around him. "Though I don't think I'm ever going to come all the way down after being with you, Mr. Mac Wild," she whispered, then dropped a soft kiss on his lips before laying her head back down on his shoulder and snuggling her face under his chin.

The guilt Mac had lived with on a daily basis since Kate died quadrupled. But taking Ashley to the stars had been what he wanted, wasn't it? Giving her a taste of the life she would have never let herself have if he hadn't shown up on her doorstep and pressed the issue?

If he'd known this was where they would end up he wouldn't have lied to her about who he was. Or would he have?

She wouldn't have wanted anything to do with him until his version of his relationship with Stephanie had been proven, and she would have disapproved of his unwillingness to do his duty toward his family. No, if he hadn't lied to her, he wouldn't have her wrapped in his arms, the heat of her naked breasts hot against his chest, even though the rest of her skin grew chilled beneath his touch. This time with Ashley was worth the guilt.

He prayed to the wide, star-filled sky and the newly risen moon that the truth wouldn't hurt her too deeply.

The need to care for her while he could spread through him like thick smoke. He gave her one last squeeze, released her, and said, "Let's get you inside."

"That's probably a good idea." She grabbed the edges of the blanket and wrapped it around herself as she sat up, pulling it part way out from underneath him.

The crisp, spring air on his bare chest after her heat tightened his skin and the scratchy roughness of the boards against his back brought a bittersweet smile to his mouth. Talk about making a memory. He sat up also and reached for their clothes. He handed Ashley her shirt and her jeans, and was rewarded with the best knowing smile he'd ever seen. His body, which by all rights should have been too pooped to pop, reacted in an instantaneous and appropriate way.

But without the other's body heat, the night air was getting damn cold and didn't encourage any more dallying. He pulled on his clothes as fast as he could and had the picnic remnants loaded back in the basket by the time Ashley was dressed. She was still shivering, so he wrapped the blanket around her shoulders. He picked up the basket and slipped the other hand behind her waist to hold her close to whatever heat he could offer her for the walk back to the house.

She snuggled against his side, matching his easy pace with her own long-legged stride. The rightness of her fit against him made his throat tight. Fortunately she seemed content not talking. The crunch of the fine gravel of the path to the veranda provided the only sound that wasn't insect generated.

They were passing beneath the great oak tree in the middle of the lawn when she turned her face up to his, her skin glowing like porcelain in the moonlight. "Let's go to my room," she said.

The image of what he'd glimpsed of her bedroom came to mind and Mac instantly rejected the idea. He didn't want all those frilly pillows and frothy bedding on the bed she had to sleep in every night to hold any haunting reminders of him after she sent him on his way.

He squeezed her waist. "Naa. Mine's already broken in. Besides, that's where the rest of my little friends are."

Her step faltered, making them bump together. "Your *little friends?*"

"The condoms."

She laughed into the corner of the blanket she held in her fist. "Ah. Then we definitely need to be where *your little friends* are. Unless, of course, you wouldn't mind making a quick, though quiet, trip to your room to bring them along while I slip into something more comfortable in mine?"

He shook his head as they mounted the veranda stairs. "Nope. Can't."

"Why not?"

"I'd trip on the *looong* string of packages I'm going to need to keep up with you tonight. No, wait." He pulled his hand from her waist and pointed a finger at her. "You're the one who's going to try to keep up with me."

Opening one of the French doors to the house, he held it for her so she could enter and punch in the security code on the alarm keypad next to the door. "Either way," he whispered, "we are going to need a lot of *my little friends.*"

"Okay, okay. Your room it is," she conceded and led the way into the kitchen to drop off the picnic supplies.

After setting down the basket, Mac went to the fridge.

"What are you after now?" she whispered, slipping the blanket from her shoulders and folding it.

"Li-quids," he pronounced succinctly. He loaded his arms with bottles of water until Ashley giggled uncontrollably. It gave him such a rush to make her so happy, and he hated the fact it had to end. But what was done was done.

Nowhere near ready to let Ashley go yet, he led her back to his room. He was far more leisurely undressing her and getting her on his bed than he had been their first time, covering every newly bared inch of skin with his lips, his hands, his reverence.

Her playful mood settled in the face of his earnestness, and she soulfully accepted what he needed to give, her hands gentle in his hair.

He showed her the things he couldn't say, the things that couldn't be.

Then he made love to her and talked to her about the world and held her through the night, free to allow her closer than any woman since Kate. Because once she saw his real name in the paper, she would want nothing more to do with him.

He'd suffer that punishment as his due. Then he'd go back to his life, haunted by the memories of two extraordinary women.

Morning found him unwilling for that depressing reality to begin yet. Mac delayed Ashley from going downstairs once, but he finally reached a point were he was physically unable to give her a decent reason to stay in bed with him any longer. She slipped from between the sheets with the promise to meet him downstairs for breakfast after she'd showered and dressed.

He seriously considered staying in bed and letting her read the paper and find out the truth by herself, but he'd never been a coward. He deserved the anger she'd unleash on him in spades.

He still had a hell of a time getting up, blaming his bone-weariness on the fact that he hadn't slept more than an hour or two the last couple of days. He moved slow enough showering and dressing in jeans and a chambray shirt—what he usually flew in—that when he finally made it downstairs, he wasn't surprised to find Ashley already at the marble breakfast table. Thanks to whatever Marie was busy whipping up on the grill, the sun-washed kitchen smelled heavenly, but Mac found he didn't have his usual appetite.

Dreading what was to come more than he'd thought possible, he paused in the doorway for a moment.

Ashley looked like a sunray come to life in a pale yellow knit hooded and zippered top over a white T-shirt with her shining blond hair pulled back in a clip. With her day planner and a phone book open before her, her slender, gold pen flashed in the morning light as she ignored the nearby grapefruit half and yogurt mixed with granola. She looked very much like the old, proper Miss Ashley Rivers.

Only the secret-sharing gleam in her blue-green eyes when she glanced up and met his gaze told him Ash Bash hadn't been entirely banished again.

And she obviously hadn't read the newspaper yet.

Damn it. It was right at her elbow, ready to be

picked up at any second. He suddenly needed to get this over with. It was like sitting in a dentist chair, knowing an infected tooth had to come out, but there was no Novocain. He'd worked himself up to this point, now he just wanted it done.

One side of her lush mouth, the mouth he'd come to know so well, curved up in a provocative smile. "Good morning, Mac." She glanced toward Marie, who had turned toward him at Ashley's greeting.

After Marie added her own good morning and turned her back to them once again to finish frying the diced potatoes he'd caught a glimpse of, Ashley looked back at him.

She waggled her elegant brows in the damnedest way. "I trust you slept well."

He swallowed the lump of burning regret in his throat and threw her a cheery-sounding line. "Like a dog who's had his belly rubbed, sunshine."

Her grin broadened. "Funny, because I slept like a well-petted cat."

Mac's heart barely withstood the unexpected blow. He didn't know why her wonderful wit still managed to surprise him. He forced a cocky smile. "I bet you did."

His gaze snagged on the thick, Sunday paper sitting on the end of the table again as he slipped into the chair directly across from her. The knot of apprehension tightened in his stomach.

Just pull the damn tooth.

He stupidly asked the obvious, "You haven't read the newspaper yet, have you?"

She didn't spare the paper a glance. "No. I've been too busy with something else."

Her expectant, almost excited gaze let him know what he was supposed to do. He complied. "Which is?"

"Well." She readjusted herself in her seat like a squirmy kid. "I've been thinking, as soon as you finish with your work for my brother, you would benefit from having some other contacts in environmental services already lined up, so that you can start on another project right away." She dropped her gaze to her day planner and her color flared. "So you won't have to leave."

So he wouldn't have to leave.

God help him, it just kept getting worse. His inevitable betrayal of her rose up like bile to choke him. He remained silent, his throat too tight to manage even a grunt.

She glanced to him quickly, then looked at the page she had the phone book open to. "I'll have whatever office equipment you'll require set up either in your suite or, if you prefer, a different room—heaven knows we have them to spare—so that you'll be all set." She met his gaze again. The hope in hers made him feel ill. "You do want to stay, don't you, Mac?"

What he wanted didn't matter. "Ashley, I...I think you should read the paper."

"Why?"

Because you'll hate me when you do and then I can go back to keeping my oath to Kate.

"Because there will probably be something about Friday night in there."

Her eyebrows shot up and her eyes went wide, then she laughed. "Oh, the banquet. I thought for a second you meant what we—that is..." She waved off her notion of the paper having covered their first sexual encounter. "Yes, there might be. But other than wanting to see Grandmother's charity work acknowledged, I don't care about that sort of thing."

He reached for the paper and flipped through it until he found the Arts and Entertainment section. Pulling it out of the stack, he extended it toward her, wanting his sham over once and for all. "I didn't think you did, but you should check it out all the same." Someone she knew undoubtedly would, and it would only be a matter of time before she found out.

She deserved to have him present to take her wrath. Almost as much as he needed to receive it.

"All right. If you insist." She took the paper and opened it, her face blocked from his view. "Oh, Mac," she said, then lowered the paper so quickly he jumped. Her smile was shy and far, far too adorable. "I keep meaning to ask you something. Do you like—that is, do you ever plan to have...children...of your own...eventually?"

Her question seared his heart. No, he didn't plan to, but planning and wanting were two different things.

He told her only part of the truth. "Kids are great, Ashley. Is there anything in there about the banquet?"

Her smile turned dreamy for a second and Mac had never felt as big a jerk in his life. He'd led her down this road, only to blow a bridge out from under her.

Her expression cleared and he knew his question had sunk in. "Oh. We had our picture taken, didn't we? I bet you've never had the opportunity to be in the newspaper, before, have you? Well, let me just take a look here..." She raised the paper in front of her face again and Mac suddenly felt like puking.

Why in the hell had he done this to her? Ashley hadn't deserved to be used for his selfish need to escape his own life, to forget for a little while. She hadn't deserved to be so led on.

She flipped a page. "Ah, here we are—oh, poop!"

Oh, poop? Out of all the possible reactions to finding out who he really was, her exclaiming *oh, poop* hadn't been one he'd expected.

She lowered the paper and looked at him apologetically. "I'm so sorry, Mac. They didn't get your name. And you can't see much of your face, either. I wish I'd realized we'd had our picture taken, but as you can see—" she turned the paper so he could see the three-by-five, black-and-white photo of him practically sticking his nose in Ashley's ear and her looking as if she enjoyed it *a lot* "—my mind was clearly on something else." She winked, then turned the paper back toward herself. "Still, it's a shame the caption only identifies you as my escort." She *tsked*. "That really won't do."

Mac barely heard her. He hadn't been identified. Ashley didn't know that her *regular guy* was actually anything but. He didn't have to leave.

Holy, flaming haggis.

But he *did* have to leave. He had an oath to fulfill, and he'd already made his heart's one commitment. No matter how much he might want otherwise, he'd allowed this to go on long enough. It looked like he'd have to pull the tooth himself.

"Ashley, there's something I have to—"

Footsteps sounded on the kitchen's flagstone-tiled floor and Ashley's face lit up when she looked over Mac's shoulder. "Dad! You're home."

Mac turned and locked gazes with George Rivers, and his breath froze in his chest.

The older man's eyebrows went up, creating rows and rows of wrinkles across his balding head. "Wilder MacDougal! Why the hell are you here and not in New York facing that paternity scandal like a man?"

Leave it to George to knock all his teeth out with one punch. But having it over with wasn't the relief Mac had thought it would be. His gaze went automatically to Ashley. The truth hadn't registered yet. But it would. The prospect made his insides shrivel and crumple like a paper tossed in the fire.

Mac decided facing a firing squad of flame-throwers would be better than having to face the confusion and the hurt that would surely follow in her beautiful, once trusting eyes.

Chapter Ten

Ashley blinked at her father, surprised he would make such a mistake. Worry forced a crease in her brow. Perhaps the schedule of charity golf tournaments she'd planned for him was too rigorous. Though still standing tall and in great shape for his age, her mother's death nearly three years ago had taken its toll.

Noting the slightly mussed appearance of his sage-green, short-sleeved golf shirt and black slacks, he'd clearly just arrived home from the airport. She searched his face for signs of fatigue, but only found the characteristic flush he gained when his formidable temper ran high and a steely hardness in his blue-green eyes as he watched Mac rise and offer her father his hand with a murmured, "George."

Mac stood taller than her father, but Mac's deferential posture put them nearly eye to eye.

"Dad. This isn't Wilder MacDougal. Though from what I've heard said about that particular gentleman's looks, he and Mr. Mac...Wild...here..." Her gaze fastened on Mac as the slight stirrings of recognition she'd had when she'd first laid eyes on him in their foyer returned with pounding intensity. While she'd never seen Wilder MacDougal in person, she had vaguely noted pictures of him in various publications and heard plenty of specifics about his perpetual bachelor status and wild streak from friends who had met him.

Realization dawned with sickening clarity and her stomach rolled. Her horrified gaze locked on Mac's topaz eyes, appearing more golden in contrast to the blue of his chambray shirt. His look of resignation provided the confirmation she needed.

And he'd just called her dad George.

Mac Wild. Wilder Huntington MacDougal V or something or other. Good Lord, the alias was so close, so obvious, so simple.

She was such a fool. The certainty ripped her heart from her chest.

She knew all about the MacDougals of New York: their ancient, strong lineage, their mind-boggling and equally ancient wealth, their willingness to spread it among numerous charities. Not to mention their current troubles with a certain socialite, whom Ashley had a passing knowledge of also, and the lady's claims made with tacky noisiness in the tabloid press.

And Ashley had been used in the worst way possible by the cause of those troubles. Hot, thick tears filled her eyes and Mac's guilty, soulful face swam. Damn him. Damn him for making her trust again, the whole time knowing everything was a lie.

Her father's voice brought her out of the hazy cloud of pain. "What the hell's going on here? Ashley? Good God—"

Mac cut off her father's warm-up to a tirade. "Mr.

Rivers, I'm afraid I have some explaining to do to your daughter. Then I'll certainly explain everything to you."

Her dad widened his stance, planted one fist on his hip, and pointed a finger at her. "Boy, judging by the look on her face—a look, I'll have you know, I have never seen before in her entire life—you had better give your explanation right here." He dropped his finger to point at the floor. "Right now, in my presence."

Having her father come to her defense flung the door shut on her hurt and opened the floodgates to anger. How dare Mac play her for a fool in front of the man she'd dedicated the past fifteen years to proving herself worthy to? She slammed her planner shut, shoved her chair back with a loud scrape and shot to her feet.

Mac addressed her father, though he seemed reluctant to take his gaze from her. He undoubtedly sensed her raging desire to remove the hair from his head and felt the need to keep his eyes on her. "I'm not in New York, sir, because Harrison generously offered me a place to stay until things settled down. And why am I not facing the scandal like a man?"

He slanted her father a look. "I don't have a defense for that, other than to say that I felt avoiding the press until the woman in question's lies become apparent was the best way to keep the media coverage to a minimum."

Stunned by his audacity, Ashley forced her voice past anger's constrictor-like squeeze on her throat. "So you're saying Stephanie Thorton-Stuart is a liar, too?"

Mac looked at her, his gaze as accusing as the finger he pointed at her, the finger that only hours before had traced a delicious path around her breast. "See, I *knew* you'd know her. And I knew you wouldn't understand."

Being pointed at like an inanimate object by both of them made her blood settle into a full boil. "You're right, Mac. I don't understand how you could come into my home, look me dead in the eye, lie to me, and—and—" she faltered, the thought of how he'd pursued her, how he'd seduced her, both body and soul, sent a sob clawing up her tight throat. Only the years of practice she'd had controlling her emotions allowed her to subdue the pitiful noise before it could escape.

She looked away, unseeing, to the window filling the room with a suddenly glaring light and pulled in several deep breaths to drive the need to wail down into her aching chest. She wouldn't break down now. She couldn't. She had to salvage something of her father's respect. He would think the worst of her if he found out how easily she'd been manipulated, how foolish she'd been.

Once she trusted her voice again, she turned her attention to her father. He was looking at her as if he'd never seen her before, his thick, once dark-blond brows low over his eyes. "Dad, could you please excuse us? I need to have a private word with Mr. Wil— Mr. MacDougal."

Her dad's frown was fierce and intimidating. And had never before been directed at her. "Exactly what has been going on here?"

"Daddy—" She stopped herself, appalled by how pitiful she sounded, how young and insecure, and took refuge in the Three P's: *Propriety, Presentation and Principle.* The last of which Mac clearly lacked. She had to remember who was at fault here.

She slowly drew herself up to her full height to face the two men with as much dignity as she could muster. "I'm afraid I drew some inappropriate conclusions based on Mr. MacDougal's desire to remain...incognito. Apparently Harrison is aware of the situation and deemed the subterfuge necessary. I simply would like to clarify a few things with Mac—Wilder—"

"It's Mac. My friends really do call me Mac."

But what did his lovers call him? Her heart curled in on itself. Maybe she didn't rate inclusion in that group. She swallowed the bitter taste of agony and willed her voice to ring with firm conviction and control. "Well, I would like to have a moment alone to speak with *Wilder.*" She refused to let him hope for one moment that nothing would change. Just as she refused to allow her own hope to survive the trust-breaching flood of his lies.

Her father pulled in a noisy breath through his nose, a sound Ashley heard often when her brother challenged his patience. He eyed her and Mac for a moment, then released the breath. "All right. But I expect to be told why in the hell you look like he torched your day planner."

Ashley drew back her chin, then looked down. At some point she'd picked up her planner and was clutching it to her chest, her knuckles white against the black leather. She eased her grip, surprised by her father's choice of disasters. Mac nodded slightly as if he shared her father's assessment of the importance of the planner. She really must be slipping to have grown so transparent.

Her father turned to leave, and Ashley noticed Marie hovering by the grill behind him, a concerned look on her face. Ashley quietly offered, "Dad, why don't you stay here and let Marie fix you something to eat. I know how you feel about airplane food. We'll go elsewhere."

He nodded and agreed gruffly, "Fine. But I'll be waiting on an explanation of what's been going on."

She pulled in a silent breath, not to gain patience, but to ward off the heart-pounding panic generated by the thought of her father learning how intimate she and Mac had become in such a short time. Glossing over most of what had happened was her only choice, and that would best be done after she'd had time to recover.

Like sometime next year.

She patted her father on the arm. "There's nothing more to tell, Dad. Mr. MacDougal had Harrison's blessing, and that's good enough, isn't it?"

Her father ran a weary hand over his balding head, stirring Ashley's concern again.

"Really, Dad, we can discuss it more if you wish later after you've had time to eat, rested a bit and had a chance to freshen up. All right?"

He blew out a sigh and waved them off. "Go."

She moved past him, but paused long enough to kiss his cheek. "I'm glad you made it home safely, Dad."

He accepted her kiss, grumbling, "And not a moment too soon."

Further humiliated by the fact that deep down she didn't share the sentiment, Ashley continued on out of the kitchen without bothering to look to see if Mac followed. The traitorous tingling of her skin told her he wasn't far behind as she walked briskly down the main hall, her heels marking an ominous cadence. His hikers were just as ominous in their silence.

She chose the formality of the study not only to make sure her mind and body stayed focused on the cold, hard fact that Mac had based their entire relationship on lies, but also because the room allowed her to place the large, solid mahogany desk between them as a barrier.

If only the mortar and stone around her heart had been as sturdy. He'd encouraged her to be her true self the whole time he was being two-faced and manipulative.

She pulled out her father's chair and sat down. In the past often conducting the business of Two Rivers Industries from home, this was a position of power for her father, and his father before him. George Rivers faced down those who opposed him—or so much as questioned him—here, and so far only Harrison had ever been called to the spot on the other side of the big desk and come away unscathed.

Having closed the study door behind him while she had taken her seat, Mac strode to the front of the desk, to the very spot she wanted him to occupy so she could test exactly how much of her father's daughter she was. Mac effectively breached the barrier she'd meant the desk to provide by placing his hands, strong fingers spread wide, on the gleaming top and leaning toward her, his expression hard and purposeful.

Her throat closed in agony and the backs of her eyes burned at how easy it was for him to get close to her.

He stared down at her for a moment, seeming to take her measure in the planes of her face. Or perhaps he merely searched for the chink in her armor he'd already pried open. His mouth no longer held the sensuous promise that had at first haunted her, then taken her to fantastic heights of ecstasy. Instead the firm line he'd pressed it into screamed his determination. But she wouldn't be swayed into believing what he'd done was acceptable or understandable, whatever his justification. Her armor had fused solid.

He finally met her gaze directly, the browns and golds muddied by the shadow of guilt and...something else. Pain, maybe? She didn't care. He hadn't been the one who'd been lied to.

"Look," he started, the deep, masculine resonance of his voice filling the room and her chest. "I know I don't deserve your forgiveness, but I do deserve to be heard out."

"Deserve?" She placed her elbows on the desk and tented her fingers as she'd seen her father do a thousand times. "Right now I can think of a number of things you *deserve*. A fair hearing isn't one of them."

"Okay. I *owe* you an explanation," he conceded.

She shook her head slowly and pressed her fingertips tightly together to keep her hands from visibly shaking. "Oh, you owe me so much more than that, Mac*Dougal*."

He blew out a breath. "Just let me tell you why I wasn't completely honest with you."

His audacity mind-boggling, her hands dropped to the dark-green blotter in front of her with a slap. "*Completely?* You weren't even *remotely* honest with me."

He pushed off from the desk and straightened his shoulders as if they carried great burdens. "I was, Ash. More than you'll ever know."

His intimate shortening of her name stung like salt poured into a wound, creating a brine in her heart that tainted everything he said. "Just leaving the minor details out like who and what you were."

He crossed his arms over his broad chest, his biceps bunching and stretching the sleeves of his blue cotton shirt. "I didn't think I could trust you not to make a stink about my being here, at best. At worst, to not let my family or Stephanie know where I was."

"Oh, heavens!" She threw up her hands. "Because both of those things would have been the right things to do, now, wouldn't they?"

He lowered his chin and had the nerve to give her an accusing stare. "I knew you'd think it would be the *principled* thing to do."

"Taking responsibility for your actions generally is."

He unfolded his arms and let them drop to his sides. "Stephanie's lying, Ash. She's not pregnant." He turned and paced to the floor-to-ceiling windows lining one wall of the study looking out on the hedge-bordered lawn. "And even if she is pregnant, I'm sure as hell not the father."

"How can you be so sure—"

He faced her again. "Because I never slept with her." The disgusted look on his face made her inclined to believe him when she hadn't thought herself capable of doing so ever again. "I'm not even sure I kissed her. I took her out a couple of times to make my mother happy, but that was it. She wasn't my type."

Ashley hated herself for the spurt of relief bordering on joy that he hadn't been intimate with the renowned beauty.

Though he'd chosen to be with me. Why? What was it about her that was different from Stephanie? Their similarities came to mind easily. She frowned in confusion. "But I'm your type? The type you'd sleep with, that is, not the type you'd trust." She couldn't help the bitterness in her voice.

He started back toward her. "I wanted to be able to trust you, Ash—"

She surged to her feet and raised a hand to ward him off on the chance he might try to round the desk and get near her. "You wanted to be able to trust me, but you spent all your time getting *me* to trust *you*." Struggling to maintain control, she blinked fast to contain the tears blurring her vision. "Do you have any idea how hard that was for me? To trust you? After what Roger—" The sob that had been making mincemeat of her throat finally broke free.

She gulped air to batter down any more. She would not cry over this man, despite the fact that his betrayal made Roger's seem a mere annoyance.

Mac did round the desk then, his expression turned

thunderous. "After Roger what? What did he do to you?"

She backed away from the protective outrage in his tone. She'd laugh if she wasn't likely to give way to hysterical crying. Hoping her voice would hold, she continued as she moved to place the desk between them again. "Roger Benton had only been interested in my money. Or more accurately, my family's money."

He let loose a disbelieving snort. "I'm sure that was just a bonus—"

"I heard him admit it with my own ears. While he was in bed with another woman, which I had the misfortune of seeing with my own eyes." She shook her head at the horror of that scene. "I don't know what was worse, hearing his betrayal or seeing it. He'd lied about his feelings for me. He didn't care about me one bit. He cared about the money. He was only using me to get his hands on our money and my connections to more."

Mac stilled, but his body virtually pulsed with visibly repressed rage. "Well, I'm sure as hell not interested in your money."

"No, I doubt that you are, having, what, a billion or so of your own?" she asked with as much sarcasm as she could muster. "No, Mac, you used me for something far worse. You used me for *sport*." Her chin started to quiver, but she couldn't stop now. He had to know how much he'd hurt her with his lies. "Probably to keep from being bored while you were stuck out here in the boonies—"

He cut her off. "I did not use you for sport."

"But you *did* use me."

"Damn it, Ashley, I didn't! I just wanted to get you to live a little, to see what you were missing by living such a repressed life."

She scoffed. "Oh, you loosened me up, all right. So much so you were able to waltz right in."

"I never intended for things to go so far, Ash. But…" He spread his hands wide, his submission obvious. "But I couldn't help it. I couldn't resist you."

Ashley's heart pulsed with hope. In self-defense, she mocked, "So you couldn't resist me. And yet you didn't think you could trust me enough to be honest. Why, Mac? Why didn't you tell me the truth once you knew where *things* were going with us?"

He worked his hands into the front pockets of his jeans, drawing her eyes to the way the denim molded to his incredible form. The muscles deep in her pelvis clenched in response. Heaven help her, he'd handed her an entry drug into life when he'd given her his body, and now she craved him like an addict.

"I couldn't risk it."

"But why?" she pleaded, desperate for any excuse that would leave her less the fool.

His shoulders went slack in their sockets. "Because my family wants me to do something I can't do."

"You can't face a scandal that, if you're telling the truth now, will be proved a lie in due time?"

"There's more to it than that."

Maybe if she understood what drove him in his choices, she'd be able to box up the entire incident and file it away deep inside where it wouldn't hurt her so much. She took a tentative step toward him. "Like what?"

When he looked away and shook his head slightly, she pressed, "Mac, tell me. Help me understand why you felt the need to lie to me."

"It doesn't matter. All that matters is that you understand I didn't use you for sport. I don't want you to ever think that."

The sincerity and concern in his tone tortured her, so she lashed out. "What, you fell helplessly in love with me?" She'd tried to sound scornful, but the hopeful thread in her voice mortified her and sent her to the spot he'd occupied in front of the windows. The tears in her eyes reduced the sunny view to a shimmering blur.

"I won't lie to you now, Ashley. It wasn't love."

The words were like blows from a sledgehammer to her chest. But what had she expected? That she really was some princess who would get to live happily ever after even though her regular guy had turned out to be a prince after all?

He continued, and she curled her shoulders in against any more blows. "And it has nothing to do with you. It's me."

She heard him move behind her, and she prayed with everything she was worth that he wouldn't try to touch her, certain she'd shatter beneath his hands.

"You see," he said, his voice sounding close by, but not close enough to touch. "There's this family legend, or curse, or whatever. I don't know exactly what to call it, only that I've heard it all my life. I've had no choice but to believe in it because of all the proof I've seen over the years, and frankly because of my own experience. Everybody else in the family believes it, too, as far as I know."

He paused for what seemed an eternity, long enough that Ashley finally turned to face him. He wore a hard mask of resignation, though his eyes hinted at the sadness she had seen there before.

Her heart stalled in the mire of dread filling her chest, waiting for his pronouncement.

He pulled in a noisy breath before saying, "A MacDougal only loves once."

Chapter Eleven

The intensity of the pain clouding Ashley's eyes sent Mac back a step as effectively as if she'd taken a swing at him. But no sucker punch could produce the answering pain tearing into his chest for hurting her so much. The blow was different from what he'd experienced after losing Kate, but no less agonizing.

Granted, Ashley's hand hadn't slipped lifeless from his, but she was still no longer in his life.

And once again, he was to blame.

The familiar guilt clogged his throat and made it hard to breathe. Once again, if he had made different choices, a wonderful, special woman wouldn't be paying the price.

He pulled his gaze from Ashley's, and as he had after Kate gave up her fight despite his begging and pleading, he grasped for the only defense available to him. He emotionally shut down, the blessed numbness coating the gash on his soul with a soothing thickness, a suffocating goo that let nothing in or out.

The numbness allowed him to return his gaze to Ashley's, her crushed spirit so clear in the tear-swollen sea of her beautiful blue-green eyes. While he could only provide her with an apology—not an explanation, for she would never be able to understand what had passed between him and Kate, the oath she'd demanded of him—his conscience demanded he remain a stationary target for the rage he prayed would come.

ASHLEY TRIED TO PROCESS the words Mac had spoken, she did, but she couldn't get past the fact that he had just admitted he would never love her, that she would never be the woman he wanted. At least, beyond the physical.

She had been sampled and rejected.

That humiliating, painful knowledge created a vortex in the center of her chest that pulled everything inside of her into its middle, sucking her slowly into oblivion. She gasped against the pull, forcing her focus outward to keep from completely dissolving.

Still staring at Mac's face, she suddenly realized the emotions passing so clearly behind his eyes before he shifted his gaze to the floor didn't corroborate his words. He didn't look like a man emotionally unaffected by their relationship. He looked deeply affected. Pain, sharp and clear, mirrored her own. She remembered seeing similar, though not nearly as intense, distress in his eyes on other occasions. If he couldn't—wouldn't—love her, then what hurt him so much? Guilt was clearly present, but there was so much more that she couldn't decipher.

Then the fleeting emotions were gone. His face settled into a mask of control, a mask of denial. Undoubtedly to allow him to cope. But with what?

Empathy for Mac's hurt doubled the size of the consuming whirlpool in her chest.

Anger erupted and filled the void. He had no right to hurt her the way he had then make her feel worse because he'd been wounded, too. She strode past him, pitifully aware that he didn't reach out for her when she came within arm's length of him. Her entire body cried out for contact with him like a flower seeking the sun. Unfortunately she knew now how deeply his heat could burn her.

Berating herself for such weakness, for still wanting him, she opened the left top drawer of her father's desk to get out a tissue. She had to regain her control.

Mac's gaze lay as heavy as a wary hand on her while she dabbed the tissue beneath her eyes. Hating that he was seeing her this way—weak and vulnerable—she turned her back on him to wipe her nose. She would not let him steal her dignity as well as her heart.

"Ashley."

She ignored his deep, and disturbingly colorless, voice. She could never deal with this, never get back to the efficient, controlled, safe place she'd been before he and his filthy bike invaded her world if she didn't present herself the best she could.

"Ashley, I'm sorry."

Her face settled in what she prayed was an equally unaffected expression, she raised her chin and turned toward him, proud that she was proving stronger than the voracious agony that was doing its best to devour her from the inside. "As well you should be. If you'll remember, I once told you that one should never enter into a relationship unless one is willing—or able, as in your curious case—to give all of oneself." She glared at him. "You should have never pursued me, Mac."

"I know, Ash. Again, I'm sorry."

She stiffened her spine to combat the heartbreaking familiarity of her shortened name on his lips. She never wanted to hear it again. "It's Ashley. Now, I really would like a more detailed explanation about what it is your family wants you to do." She reached for her planner on the desk and opened it.

As fate would have it, she'd opened to the page bearing her list of supplies to order so she could set up an office here at the house for Mac's *Environmental Specialist* job. She sniffed delicately. What a fool she'd been. The man in actuality owned his own multimillion-dollar financial corporation of some sort, on top of his family's ancient wealth.

She tore the page from the book. Ash-Bash would crumple the paper into a ball, vault over the desk and slam-dunk the wad down Mac's throat. Instead Ashley folded it neatly and bent to deposit it into the wastebasket beneath the desk. "Perhaps I can help."

"You can't help, Ash—Ashley."

"Once again, you underestimate me, Mac." And offended and hurt and confused her to her very core. The vortex whirled, but she held strong against it.

Propriety, Presentation and Principle.

She would survive this. She would survive this just as she'd survived her father's disapproval, Roger's betrayal and her mother's death. Though truly, this was the only thing that had come close to the pain she'd felt when her mother died.

She shut her day planner and scooped it up. "Since you aren't willing to be any more forthcoming regarding your situation, I suppose we're done. I need to attend to some things that I've neglected the past day or two."

While I lay in your arms believing we could have a future together.

The vortex stole her breath for a moment, but she forced her lungs to fill so she could continue with what she needed to say. "If I don't, my father will suspect that everything is not all right after all." Proud of how calm and strong she sounded, she rounded the desk and headed for the door.

His voice stopped her. "But it's not all right, is it?"

Slowly she turned around and met his flat, simply hazel gaze. "It has to be, Mac. You've made that abundantly clear." She started again for the door, but a thought occurred to her. Pausing, she looked at him again. "At least tell me why you chose to come here, to our home. Surely there were other places you could have slinked off to."

He shrugged slightly. "I guess the idea of hiding in Plainview appealed to me."

His answer was so...Mac. She closed her eyes against the swell of pain.

"I'm sorry it has to be this way, Ashley."

Her heart, lost somewhere in the growing hole inside of her, wept. But she didn't. "So am I, Mac. So am I."

He didn't say another word as she left the study.

His silence closed the door on any hope she might have harbored that there could be a chance for them as effectively as the door she pulled shut behind her.

He really didn't want her.

Unwilling to rouse her father's suspicion any more than it already was if she happened to bump into him on her way to her room, she stopped in the downstairs powder room to check her makeup. Her reflection made her pause. Her mascara hadn't run and her nose held only a hint of red, but she looked different. Her eyes glittered hard, refracting the light the same way the cut crystal globes over the mahogany-framed mirror did.

She looked like Ash-Bash.

Mac had done a fine job of reawakening the girl she'd once been. Heaven help her deal with the woman she'd become.

A woman who would never love again.

She thankfully made it back to her room without running into her father, who was probably about done with his breakfast, or her grandmother, who would be returning from church at any time. Ashley locked the outer door to her suite with every intention of heading for her bed and burying herself deep beneath the covers. At least she and Mac hadn't made love there. She didn't think she could bear lying in a bed that held such memories.

Memories of her gripping the sheets as the rough pads of his fingers—earned not by taking soil samples or turning over rocks searching for oil traces as she'd thought, but by rock climbing or something equally pointless—traced over her sensitized, vulnerable skin.

Memories of her turning her face into a soft pillow to muffle her cry of pleasure, the finely spun cotton of the pillowcase cool on her flushed cheeks. She squeezed her eyes shut and forced the images away. At least her bed wouldn't hold those memories. If only her mind didn't.

As she passed her desk and set down her day planner, her Rolodex caught her eye. She remembered Mac commenting that she must have the number of the entire free world indexed there. He'd undoubtedly figured she had a MacDougal or two listed in it, or perhaps even Stephanie Thorton-Stuart herself.

Ashley didn't, but she certainly knew someone who did. Her mind exploded with possibilities.

Perhaps if she could learn enough to gain some understanding of Mac, learn why he hurt and why he was so willing to hurt her, she'd be able to plug the swirling hole in her chest. She sat down at her desk, then hesitated. It would be going against propriety to pry.

Should she care anymore?

Ashley propped her elbows on the desk and cradled her aching head in her hands. She didn't even know who she was anymore, let alone what she should do. If only her mother were here to help her through this. She hadn't sought her mother's advice after Roger's betrayal, or so much as told her about it, because Ashley had known exactly what needed to be done.

That certainly wasn't the case this time. Right now she could use Elizabeth Rivers's unfailing sensibility and calm purpose. If only her mother had been stronger than her breast cancer. Ashley missed her so much she ached.

She lifted her head from her hands and sat back in her chair. Staring at the phone, she wondered if Mac missed any of his family, if the *they're there and I'm here* comment he'd made down on the dock had only stemmed from the disagreement he was having with them about what he should do. How could he walk away from his family, from his mother, like he had? Didn't he realize how lucky he was to still have his mother? The woman was probably worried sick about him.

Ashley sat forward with a blast of purpose, suddenly certain what the *proper* thing to do was. She reached for the phone. Two calls later, with minimum name-dropping, she had Mac's mother, Mary MacDougal, on the line.

"Mrs. MacDougal, my name is Ashley Rivers. Your son Mac—that is, Wilder—is friends with my brother, Harrison, having attended Harvard together."

"Why, yes! Hello!" The older woman's voice was melodious without the slightest trace of pretension.

Ashley relaxed considerably.

"I know your grandmother and parents, myself. I was so, so sorry to hear of your mother's passing, dear. She was such a lovely, generous person."

With Ashley's emotions already scrapped raw, her eyes instantly welled with tears at the unexpected sympathy. "Yes, she was, thank you." Her mother would have undoubtedly helped Ashley avoid her current heartbreak. To regain control, she opened her day planner and penned herself a note.

Send Mac's mother a thank-you card for kind words about Mom.

Mrs. MacDougal's voice deepened with caring. "How is everyone?"

Before Ashley had a chance to answer the question, Mrs. MacDougal exclaimed, "Oh, Ashley, has your family, by any chance, heard from Wilder recently? He's...ah..." She hesitated, undoubtedly unwilling to divulge too much information regarding her son's behavior. But a mother's worry was very evident in her tone.

Ashley had done the right thing calling.

Mrs. MacDougal cleared her throat delicately, then plunged in. "He's been out of touch for some time, and I have to admit we're quite concerned about him."

Ashley leaned her elbows on the desk. "Actually, that's why I'm calling. I...we...have had—" she was as equally unsure of how much to divulge, at least until she was given some answers "—contact—" she winced at the euphemism "—with Wilder this week—"

"Praise the saints. How is he? Is he all right? He hasn't been doing anything crazy or dangerous again, has he?"

"Well, no." Aside from seducing his friend's little sister. Though he couldn't have done anything if she hadn't allowed him to. "He's fine." The image of Mac's haunted, and definitely stubborn, expression came to mind, strengthening Ashley's determination to get some answers. She sat back in her chair. "But I have to admit that the reason I'm calling you is that I'm concerned about him, also."

"Oh, no. I told his father we were pushing too hard with this whole Stephanie mess. I mean, we did believe him when he said she wasn't being entirely truthful."

Ashley raised her brows. A woman was either pregnant or she wasn't. There wasn't a lot of room for partial truths. "Wilder did mention something about you wanting him to do something he couldn't do..."

"We wanted him to marry her."

Ashley squeezed her eyes shut tight and struggled with all she was worth against the devouring mass in her chest. His parents wanted him to marry another woman. Did they think Stephanie was the one their son could love?

Mrs. MacDougal answered the silent question. "They seem such a good match, travel in the same social circles. We thought that they'd be able to get on successfully despite Wilder having already found whom he believed to be his one love."

Ashley's eyes jerked open. His one love? He'd already found her? Jealousy flared in her blood like a gas-doused flame. God help him if he was still with this woman, if he'd lied, also, about having made a commitment to someone.

"We do so want him to settle down, to stop taking such chances, that we ignored his protests, thinking it might be an excellent opportunity to help him put the past to rest and move on with his life."

Ashley struggled to process what Mrs. MacDougal was saying. So Mac hadn't declared that he couldn't love her because she wasn't the right woman for him, but because he'd already found his one true love. Then the comment Harrison had made about Mac losing someone in college flashed in her brain. "Did he love a girl who...who died?"

"Yes. Her name was Kate Wilson. She was a lovely, fun-loving girl from a wonderful family. Though not Scottish, much to my husband's chagrin." Mrs. MacDougal scoffed softly, sadly.

Ashley dropped her chin at the additional strike against her. Good thing she hadn't held out any hope for her and Mac. There wasn't a drop of Scottish blood in her entire lineage.

"They'd gone together for three years in college before she tragically died after a car accident. I'm afraid my son blames himself, despite the fact he wasn't with her when it happened."

The sadness and regret were clear in the older woman's voice. "He took her loss very badly, almost not making it through Harvard after adopting an extremely wild and often dangerous lifestyle. One he unfortunately still indulges in, and it's been over ten years since Kate died. Though he has always met all his obligations and has been extremely successful in business, which does little for our arguments that he needs to settle down."

Mrs. MacDougal heaved a sigh that rang with frustration. "All his father and I want is for him to be safe and to move on with his life. Wilder, I'm afraid, sees it otherwise."

Ashley remembered the bitterness in his tone when he spoke of his parents wanting him to do something he didn't want to do. "I'm afraid he does."

"If he had really fathered a child with Stephanie,

that would be different, of course. And I don't doubt for a second that my son would have been willing to do the right thing, then. But as time has passed and it's becoming clear to everyone that what Stephanie is claiming to be true is not the case, if you could, would you please tell Wilder we'd never force him to do something as important as getting married against his will? Despite the fact that we...well, allowed Stephanie to make some wedding plans. But please tell him the choice is his and his alone."

Mrs. MacDougal's pleading tone would have broken Ashley's heart if it weren't already long gone. Learning of Mac's past only made it worse, not better.

"We'd only thought he'd needed a push to take a step forward with his life." Mrs. MacDougal gave a wry laugh that reminded Ashley of Mac's. "He's already made it abundantly clear we made a terribly wrong assumption."

"I think, Mrs. MacDougal—"

"Oh, please, dear, call me Mary."

Warmed by his mother's kindness and at the same time saddened because Ashley wouldn't have reason to know Mary further, she said, "Thank you. I think, Mary, it would be best if he heard it straight from you."

"I've tried to contact him, but after the last time I called and urged him to consider giving Stephanie a chance, he hasn't turned his phone back on."

Ashley pinched the bridge of her nose as the memory of the name on Mac's caller ID, *M. MacDoug*, made her head throb. Everything made sense, now. "How about if I get him on the line right now?"

"You're with him?" The hope in her voice made the backs of Ashley's eyes burn again.

"He's with us. Here at our home in Oregon."

"Clear out in Oregon? Holy haggis, he *was* determined to get away from us, wasn't he?"

Ashley smiled bittersweetly at the familiar phrase. "I think he just needed some space, Mary."

"Well, the breadth of an entire country certainly qualifies."

The breadth of an entire country. If only that's all that would separate her and Mac if he did as she hoped he would and returned home to mend his relationship with his family. But there would always be so much more between them. His lies. Her hurt. His past love.

It was too much to bear.

Calling on her best social secretary voice, she said into the phone, "If you could hold for a few minutes, Mary, I'll go downstairs and get Mac on the line— forgive me, I mean Wilder."

"That's all right, dear. I know he prefers to be called Mac. In our family, the confusion between the generations of Wilders is solved by nicknaming every other generation Hunter. My husband is that generation. Our son feels that only his grandfather should be referred to as Wilder, but since he passed on, there's no point." Mary laughed, but the sound lacked much mirth. The sigh that followed rang truer over the phone line. "I will eternally be in your debt, Ashley."

"Not at all, Mary. I believe family is the most important thing in our lives."

"That and true love, dear."

"Yes," Ashley croaked as a sob rose up into her throat. "Hold, please," was all she could get out.

She fumbled for the hold button through tear-blurred vision, then gasped for air for a few moments until she had a grip on herself. While she didn't want to keep Mary waiting, she couldn't go to Mac like this. She had to make him think she was back in control, that what had passed between them hadn't devastated her.

As soon as her vision cleared and her breathing calmed, Ashley left her room in search of Mac. She looked first where she had left him in the study, but he wasn't there. Nor was he in the formal living room, dining room, or library. Dreading the possibility that Mac and her father were together in the kitchen, with Mac revealing her foolishness under her father's strident questioning, she peeked into the large kitchen. Thankfully only Marie was in there, cleaning up after Dad's breakfast. Her father must have taken her advice and gone upstairs to rest after he ate.

Ashley was about to head back upstairs to Mac's suite when she noticed him sitting out on the veranda, staring off toward the river. She fervently prayed he hadn't already spoken to her father. The less that was said between those two, the better. She'd never be able to minimize Mac's deception in her father's eyes if more was made of it than necessary. If she lost her father's respect and approval—which would cost her his love—because he thought her easily duped, she'd have to flat-out kill Mac.

Yet on the heels of her thoughts of mayhem, she

wondered if he was sitting out there thinking about her. Remembering how it had felt to be with her.

Or was he wishing she'd been Kate?

Even as the pain swirled around her like a rushing wave and soaked her to her core, Ashley slapped away the thought and grabbed the cordless handset from the phone on one of the narrow tables set periodically along the hall. She went out onto the large deck through the nearest set of French doors and marched right up to Mac's side.

He didn't look at her.

Firmly telling herself she hadn't expected or wanted him to throw himself at her feet begging for forgiveness, she pressed the button beneath the blinking light and thrust the phone in front of his face. "It's for you."

He looked from the phone to her. Although his sun-streaked, dark-brown hair was mussed, his eyes were clear, the lines of his face hard. Having ridiculously hoped his eyes would be at least a little red-rimmed and his mouth a little downturned, Ashley grit her teeth and nodded toward the phone again.

"Who is it?" he asked with unveiled suspicion.

For the first time in her life, Ashley lied without compunction. "Harrison."

As revenge went, it was a pitiful thing. Especially considering the good that would come from Mac healing his relationship with his family, but it gave her a tiny measure of satisfaction.

Mac took the phone and placed it to his ear, his gaze back on the sun-washed lawn. "Hey," he said.

She knew the second his mother spoke, because

Mac's gaze flew to hers, his eyes widening with the dawning realization of her betrayal.

Ashley didn't stick around for the hurt, then the anger that would follow. As she was sure a guy like Mac would say, *been there, done that.*

Chapter Twelve

Ashley wants me gone.

It was all Mac could think of. Even as his mother apologized in a way he'd never heard her do before for driving him clear to Oregon to escape their meddling. She practically begged him to understand why she and his father had made the mistakes they had regarding Stephanie.

Stunned by how quickly Ashley had acted to oust him from her life, he glanced to where she'd stood at his side, but she was already heading toward the French doors. She didn't turn to look at him as she went into the house, her head held high and shoulders squared beneath her pale yellow, hooded top.

He closed his eyes as his heart sunk yet further into the pit he'd dug for himself. Ashley could have simply kicked him out, telling him she didn't want to have to look at his face anymore, but her obsessive belief in family duty had her telling his mom where he was, instead.

Exactly as he'd feared she would when he'd first arrived at the Rivers's estate.

They had come full circle, with nothing more to

show for the journey than aching hearts and enough memories to haunt them for the rest of their lives.

"Wilder, honey?" His mom's voice brought his attention back to the phone he still held to his ear.

He slumped back in the padded wooden chair and rubbed a hand over his gritty eyes. "Yeah, Mom."

"So can you forgive us?"

The pleading in her tone made him sick to his stomach. Mary MacDougal should never have to plead for anything. She'd always earned every loyalty and ounce of affection that came her way. And he had a feeling his dad wasn't close enough to hear her beg, or Mac would be getting an earful of his dad yelling in the background about a thankless kid who needed his hide tanned. The image was a comforting one. "Of course."

"Then will you consider coming home?"

Mac shoved his hand through his hair. "Look, Mom, my taking off wasn't about punishing you, or anything. I just thought it would be better for me to disappear to keep the arguing and media hoopla to a minimum. After all, I knew time would make my argument for me. Has Stephanie 'fessed up to the truth, yet?"

"No, she hasn't. But she hasn't been persisting that you need to do the right thing and marry her quite so publicly, anymore. Though I've heard she did purchase a wedding dress and was looking into possible reception sites."

"I wish you hadn't sided with her on this."

"I know, dear. And again, I'm sorry. We all just want you happy and safe."

Mac shook his head at his mom wanting the two things for him he could never promise her.

"And we want you here. Would you be willing to come back home?" Before he could answer, she added, "You know, speaking of weddings, your cousin Cory's wedding is next Saturday. He would really appreciate you being there."

Sick to death of the whole mess, and worse, unable to further face the hurt he'd caused Ashley or the answering pain in his own heart, Mac latched on to an excuse to end this particularly unpleasant chapter in his life. An excuse to go home. "Yeah. I can be there for Cory's wedding. I feel bad for being so caught up in my own problems that I would have missed it."

"Everyone understands, honey. Do you need me to send the jet?"

"No. I can get back on my own. But thanks anyway."

"Wilder?"

"Yeah, Mom."

"I love you."

The numbing salve coating his heart slipped a little. "Love you, too. And I'm sorry I worried you."

"I'm the one who's sorry. Call me when you know your flight information."

"I will. Bye, Mom."

"Oh, and Wilder? Tell Ashley thank you for me. She sounds like a very good friend to you. I'll talk to you soon. Bye."

Consumed by the struggle to keep his emotions as numb as possible, Mac muttered some sort of agreement and a goodbye before turning off the phone. Ashley was a lot of things to him, but she would not appreciate being referred to as his friend.

Harrison, on the other hand, *was* his friend, and Mac hated the thought of leaving before Harrison and his wife and son returned. But actually, when he thought about it, leaving now was for the better. He wouldn't have to come up with an excuse for not attending Nathan's christening. Going to his cousin's wedding would be bad enough.

Nothing like seeing two people in love, starting their lives together with joy, hope and the support of their families to make a guy wish for what might have been in his own life. And he had the added bonus of getting to wonder what life would have been like with Ashley, too.

But he'd given Kate his word, and there was nothing he could do about it.

Mac pushed himself to his feet and started inside. There was no point delaying gathering his gear and leaving. Ashley surely didn't want to talk to him again. She'd made her feelings damn clear by dropping a dime on him and telling his mom where he was. She knew he'd either have to go home or take off for somewhere else to hide out.

And if he tried to talk to her one more time, who knew what might slip out of his mouth, how he might further damn himself by revealing what he shouldn't.

That she was the only woman to ever make him regret meeting Kate first.

ASHLEY DIDN'T KNOW that Mac had left until she discretely inquired if Donavon had provided Mac with a tray when her prayers had apparently been answered and he'd failed to appear at dinner.

"He's gone?" she stupidly repeated Donavon's words, undoubtedly revealing too much to her father and grandmother sitting at the dinner table with her.

"Yes." Donavon nodded as he placed the plate of wild greens in front of her. "He said there were things that needed his attention back home, so he was catching a flight to New York early this afternoon."

She reflexively checked her watch. At seven in the evening, Mac was probably across the country already.

Across the country and out of her life.

She should be glad. She should. With any luck he was returning to his family to heal the rift between them. His mother deserved to have her son back home and safe. But the maelstrom in her chest hadn't allowed her to feel much of anything all day beyond the slow and steady pain of being hollowed out.

Earlier, she had tried to busy herself working on Nathan's christening, but thoughts of Mac were so tied up with the ceremony that she found the task a source of pain rather than distraction. So she had immersed herself in reorganizing her office, unwittingly reaffirming her existence. Or at least, trying to.

Her grandmother said, "That is indeed a shame. I was hoping we'd have Mac's company for a while longer."

Compelled to explain, but having every intention of doing so as sketchily as she had earlier for her father, Ashley started, "Grandm—"

Her father cut her off. "I, for one, am glad he realized skulking around here instead of facing the music for his behavior back in New York was the right thing to do."

Her grandmother rolled her eyes. "Oh, pish, George. You know as well as anyone that if young Wilder had really left the Thorton-Stuart girl in the family way he would have done right by her. I personally think the boy had every right to dive for cover, and I have to admit I was pleased to walk into this dining room the other week and find him standing here." She leaned to the side to allow Donavon to serve her. "It's a pity that girl received as much attention as she did. Everyone knows she's been groomed by her parents to troll for a rich husband since she hit puberty."

Her ears ringing, Ashley gaped at her grandmother. "You knew? You knew who Mac was from the very beginning? Why didn't you tell me? Why didn't you—" She cut herself off when she caught sight of her father's increasing frown out of the corner of her eye.

Her grandmother shrugged slightly, not a trace of contrition to be found amongst the soft wrinkles on her face. She dropped her attention to attacking her salad with precision and grace. "I was well aware of the boy's reasons for wanting to hide out, and I saw no harm in it."

No harm? Ashley bit back a gasp as the whirlpool in her chest finally collapsed in on itself, leaving her with nothing more than a raw, burning ache inside. Oh, there'd been harm, all right, and Ashley had walked right into it, none the wiser.

That's not true, a voice in her head chided. *You*

knew exactly how dangerous that man would be to you, but you took him on, anyway.

She had to admit she'd wanted the adrenaline rush he gave her, the incredible feeling of being alive again. From the first moment she'd looked into his glowing, topaz eyes, she'd known he would touch her in a way no man had, and she'd wanted a taste of what he offered. She should have known, however, that one taste of a wild man would lead straight to addiction. An addiction that would leave her a hollow shell of her former self, aching for a fix of the man who had looked beyond her facade of Propriety, Presentation and Principle and spotted the true woman inside.

And had wanted her.

She would always secretly thank him for that.

Ashley glanced again at her father, who eyed her speculatively. Straightening her shoulders even though there was no longer anything left inside her to support them, she smiled in agreement. "You're right. I'm just not accustomed to being caught unprepared." Though she was growing painfully accustomed to being used. Roger had been her introductory course, and Mac had given her a Ph.D.

As soon as she finished chewing a bite, Grandmother said, "Harrison is going to be disappointed that his friend won't be here for Nathan's christening ceremony." Her already tiny shoulders drooped. "I do wish they'd get home. I'm missing my great-grandbaby horribly."

Guilt slammed into Ashley. She'd even let her brother down by driving Mac away, by becoming involved with him in the first place. She should have never let her focus stray from her commitment to her family.

She sent her grandmother an understanding smile. "They'll be home Thursday, Grandmother."

Ashley had until then to wipe the mistakes she had made from her mind and to funnel her energies into making Nathan's christening the best it could possibly be. And in the process, somehow find a way to come to terms with the fact that there would be no babies of her own to christen.

Because the only man she could ever imagine having children with was gone from her life for good.

THE WEEK INCHED BY, and no matter how much work she found to do, she couldn't wipe the memories of Mac's words, his kiss, his touch, from her mind. He hadn't simply opened the doors inside of her that she'd kept locked to be the kind of daughter her father wanted, Mac had removed them from their hinges. No matter how hard she tried, she couldn't go back to the woman she'd been before he arrived. Not completely, not after the way he'd challenged her.

She finally had to admit that it was for the better. She was a stronger woman for having known him. She'd found a way to blend the two extremes she'd lived into a complete woman. A woman who had tasted her brand of heaven and found herself miserable without it.

By the end of the week she had to admit she missed him. God, how she missed him.

Despite her efforts to cling to the hurt caused by his lies, empathy took its place as the pieces fell together.

With the added insight of his loss, the more she thought about what he'd said, what he'd done since he'd come into her life, the more she began to understand. The more she began to care.

This new caring went so much deeper than what she'd felt while lying in his arms, fantasizing about a future together, because now she understood him. And the words he had spoken to her on the basketball court took on new meanings, new depths.

With every phone call she made for her father, every order she placed for the christening ceremony, she kept hearing him challenge her about her choices, about the role she'd created for herself to play for the rest of her life.

So she *was* her family's social secretary. At least she was needed. Only not in the way she yearned to be needed. Or by the one person she had wanted more than she has ever wanted anything.

When Harrison, Juliet and Nathan returned, bursting with stories and hours of video footage of their wonderful adventures at several theme parks, Ashley's soul rebelled against the thought that she would never forge such bonds or generate such memories with a family of her own.

A loud voice in her head shouted out that she wanted what Harrison and Juliet had. Then the rest of her joined in until she wanted it with all her being.

And no matter how hard she tried, she couldn't dispute the fact that the only person on this earth she wanted it with was Mac. Despite the lies, despite the hurt, despite his past love. Despite the fact that he believed he could only love once.

By Friday afternoon as she sat at her father's desk updating his calendar and remembering all that had been said in that room, she couldn't shake the notion that Mac needed to be healed. He needed to be shown that he could find happiness again, that he *had* found it with her, for a short time, at least.

It was something she could help him with. Ashley latched on with all her might to the thought, which continued to grow and swell with possibilities. She could go to New York and convince him to give them a chance.

Maybe, over time, she could help him see that it was possible for a MacDougal to love twice in one lifetime.

Determination filled the aching void inside of her. She snatched up the phone and dialed one of the airlines, asking for flight times to New York.

Her father's voice from the doorway startled her. "New York? Who's going to New York?" His frown made clear that he better not be the one as he came into the study. Though he didn't have a golf game scheduled that day, he was still dressed in one of his favorite white golf shirts and black slacks.

"Ah." She fumbled, uncertain how to explain what she intended to do. She stalled by holding up a hand then writing down the flight times as they were given to her over the phone. She thanked the woman and hung up the phone. Meeting her father's formidable gaze, she said, "I am, actually."

His frown was swept away by a look of pleasant surprise. "Really? Why?"

"There's a...a friend of mine that I'd like to go see."

"Really?" he repeated, as if she never went anywhere.

Which certainly wasn't true. She'd traveled all over the world with her family, just not much on her own lately.

He sat down with a soft groan in one of the chairs facing the desk then gave her a patriarchal smile. "Glad to hear it, Ashley. Damn glad to hear it. You don't go off and do things for yourself enough these days. When are you leaving?"

She glanced down at the daily flight times she'd been given. One left Portland later that very night. She'd have more than enough time to make the drive up there, or she could even take a commuter flight from Eugene to Portland. Either way, she figured the sooner the better. Before she lost her nerve. "Tonight, I guess."

Her father sat forward, his brows high. "Tonight? Why? You'd barely get there before you'd have to hop right back on an airplane to get home before Nathan's christening ceremony Sunday."

Stunned, Ashley slumped back in the big leather chair. How could she have forgotten Nathan's christening?

"You forgot?" Disbelief brought her father's pitch up a notch. Then he narrowed his eyes at her. "This friend you were planning on seeing wouldn't happen to be a certain wily MacDougal, would it?"

Ashley's face heated. Even his mere name could make her blush.

Her father sat back and slapped a hand down on the arm of his chair. "I knew it! I knew there'd been something going on between you two. Mother wouldn't admit to knowing anything, but I knew something was up."

Shamed by how stupid she had been to even entertain the thought of going after Mac, especially with the christening in two days, she protested, "Dad—"

"So why did it take damn near a week for you to realize you needed to go after him?"

Certain she'd misunderstood, she leaned forward. "Excuse me?"

"Why did you take so long to decide to fight for him?"

"I never implied that I intend to—"

"Well, you should. You two are exactly what the other needs. He needs a, er, calming influence, and you sure as hell could use some loosening up."

Ashley blinked in astonishment. "What? *Dad!*"

"Do you need any help packing? Your grandmother must be hanging around here somewhere." He shot out of the chair and headed for the door. "I'll tell Donavon you need a ride to the airport. We'll charter you a plane to take you up to Portland, so you'll have plenty of time to catch the flight to New York."

Ashley leapt to her feet, terror that her father might be shoving her out because of her foolishness over Mac making her heart pound. "Dad. I'm not going."

He stopped. "Why the hell not?"

She slowly closed her day planner. While she knew she could never completely go back to how she was before, no one else need know that. "I can't. Not with Nathan's christening this weekend."

He marched back toward the desk. "Oh, no. You were already planning to go—"

"I'd forgotten, just for a moment, about the christening. I can't leave and risk not making it back." She was still needed. She still had a job to do for her family and couldn't risk letting them down more than she already had.

"Oh, yes, you can. And you will. Everyone, Harrison and Juliet especially, will understand if you don't make it back, which you shouldn't even attempt to do."

Ashley gripped the edge of the desk, trying to steady herself against the sensation of things rapidly spinning out of her control. "But there's so much that needs to be done, caterers to be coordinated—"

"All of which somebody else can handle."

She tightened her hold on the desk until her knuckles turned white. What her father was proposing threatened her very existence. "But it's my job to—"

Her father slapped a hand down on the desk and Ashley jerked back.

"It is *not* your job. It has never been your job to take care of every little thing involving this family." He ripped the world as she knew it right out from under her, then pulled in a deep breath in an obvious effort to calm himself. "Listen, sweetheart, I admit that it made life much easier for me when you stepped up and took over running things after your mother died, and I did get kind of used to it. But I never intended caring for this family to be your life's work. Hell, you've made it your entire life."

He came around the desk and held out his hands to her, the eyes she shared softened with caring. "That's not right, honey. I want more for you than that."

Her eyes clouding with tears from her father's unexpected sentiments, Ashley took his hands, "But I want to contribute something to this family. I want to be an asset to you."

He squeezed her hands, then pulled her into his arms for the first time in years. "You are, Ashley. You always have been. I've always been so proud of my strong little girl. And I'll love you no matter what you do." He pulled back and looked into her eyes, conviction and love shining in his gaze. "But I *do* want you to get on a plane tonight and fly to New York."

She opened her mouth to protest, thinking that after the christening would be soon enough. Her father stopped her with a shake of his head, capturing her face between his hands. "It can't wait. I read somewhere in one of the financial papers that there's a MacDougal wedding scheduled for tomorrow."

A bomb with the force to shatter Ashley's world went off in her head. Mac's mother's words reverberated in the blast's echo. *We wanted him to marry her.*

But Mac had said he wouldn't—couldn't do it. Had he changed his mind to help heal the rift with his family? Even as her heart screamed no, her brain rejected the idea. It couldn't be.

She pulled out of her father's grasp. "No. Mac wouldn't...he doesn't even like her...he—"

"I don't think you should chance it, girl. Your

grandmother and I will see to any last-minute details for the christening. And if I know you, you've already arranged to have it videotaped, so you won't miss a thing."

She nodded weakly. He was right. She had arranged for a videographer to record the ceremony. He did know her. Just as Mac had. And her father was right about one other thing: she couldn't risk the wedding not being Mac's. She couldn't let him marry someone else without first giving the two of them a chance.

Her dad gave her a gentle, knowing smile, one she hadn't seen since before her mother's death. Gesturing toward the door, he said, "Now, go."

Unsure whether to laugh or cry from his newfound support, she picked up her day planner and started for the door.

No. You don't need it.

Ashley paused. This time it wasn't Mac's voice in her head. It was her own, her true self. Ashley realized that she should leave the planner, that she should let go of what it represented. She needed to go after Mac without her shield, her safety line. The planner had come to define her position in her world, a physical manifestation of her worth. Thanks to Mac, she knew she was worth a lot more.

She turned back to her father and held the black leather notebook out to him. "Here. You might need a number or two out of this."

His gaze jumped from the planner to her eyes, his surprise clear. She could tell he understood she was willing to leave the planner for more than just what it contained.

She nodded her reassurance, and his surprise gave way to a pride that warmed her to her soul when he reached for the planner. Her hand only trembled slightly when she gave it to him.

"That's my girl. Have a safe trip."

Her smile was much stronger, though, as she started toward the door again, because she really didn't need the day planner. She *was* her father's strong little girl. *Hell,* as he used to say, *she was Ash Bash.*

And Mac better not be the one getting married, or there'd be hell to pay.

ASHLEY DOZED FITFULLY on the flight to New York, arriving painfully aware of why they call the particular flight she'd taken the red-eye. But if a bedraggled appearance was enough to affect her chances with Mac, then she'd made yet another grave error when it came to men.

Since she wasn't certain what the next few hours held for her, or if Mac was even in New York, she didn't want to get a hotel room. She wanted to see Mac first, find out what sort of battle she had ahead of her to convince him to give them a chance. Climbing into a cab at the airport, she gave the cabbie the address for MacDougal House from the index card she'd only last week added to her Rolodex.

The ride was long and nerve-racking. The traffic seemed thicker, the lights seemed to stay red longer than the last time she'd been to New York with her family. But being there to see shows and to shop was a far cry from chasing after a man. Try as she may, she couldn't stop herself from mentally rehearsing what she'd say to him, and her speech never came out right.

The home the cab pulled up to left her open-mouthed and praying she hadn't made a mistake. The white stone mansion rising behind a matching, high wall resembled the most aristocratic of châteaus in the Beaux Arts style, with high, ornately finished peaks and richly carved stone sills on every window.

In comparison, the Rivers's estate looked like a tract house. And to think her heart had twisted for Mac when she'd believed he felt overwhelmed by the grandeur of the awards banquet.

She allowed herself a loud snort before she approached the security booth, gave her name to the doorman and asked to see Wilder MacDougal V.

The doorman, impeccably uniformed in a long, dark-blue, double-breasted coat with gold buttons and braid, very politely informed her that Wilder MacDougal the younger, along with the rest of the family, had already left for St. Patrick's Cathedral.

Ashley yanked up her leather coat sleeve to expose her watch. It was only ten o'clock! Who in their right mind scheduled a wedding for ten o'clock in the morning?

The blood roared through her veins along with the answer. Only people who were getting married with less than a week's notice.

Chapter Thirteen

Mac blew out a breath, then shifted on the hard pew and readjusted the hem of his kilt to allow for more airflow. The ceremony had barely started and already he was too hot and too damn uncomfortable.

Despite the cavernous size of the old cathedral, every one of the thousand or so guests wanted to be as close to the front as possible to witness the union of his apparently very popular younger cousin and the lovely bride.

All those bodies coupled with the sun shining colorfully through the huge stained-glass windows and glinting off white marble columns generated a lot of heat on a warm spring morning. His formal Scottish attire, a fitted black jacket and a kilt in the MacDougal vibrant red, green and purple tartan—a getup he normally felt very comfortable in—weighed hot and oppressive on him, and the smell of damp wool was giving him a headache.

He pinched the bridge of his nose and acknowledged the heat wasn't the real reason he wished he was anywhere other than a church in the midst of a marriage ceremony. He'd hoped he was still numb enough to weather this particular celebration of life and love, a celebration he would never personally partake in. But his insides were twisting with so much regret and frustration he could hardly stand it.

He'd made so many mistakes with both Kate and Ashley, he didn't have a clue where to begin to ask for forgiveness from the carved saints lining the walls.

And the absolute, most godawful part was that when the bride had walked past him on her way to the altar, Mac hadn't imagined Kate in the place of Cory's bride. Guilt rolled through him because he'd envisioned Ashley in all her elegant, damn near regal glory, with her silky blond hair pulled back from her beautiful face and her deep, blue-green eyes bright with hope and joy. She'd make the most stunning bride on earth.

But not his bride.

Mac wanted to throw back his head and howl in pain and impotent rage and jealousy.

Instead he yanked his jacket down over the white cuff of his shirt. He'd made his choice when he'd given his word to Kate, and there was nothing he could do about it now but pray Ashley got over her hurt and went on. He had to keep telling himself that he hoped she found some guy who would see through her icy efficiency to her true, fiery self. A man who would love the real Ashley the way she deserved to be loved.

A man who loved her the way he did.

The admission delivered a gut-punch that bent him in half. He covered it by reaching down to fiddle with his leather sock garter. When he regained his breath and straightened back up, out of the corner of his eye he caught his mother, seated on his right next to the aisle, staring at him.

Her brown eyes, darkened by the cream silk suit she wore, were sharp and assessing. He raised his chin and tried to look bored.

Inside, he admonished himself for putting that particular label on the feelings he had for Ashley. It wasn't possible for him to love her. Kate had been his one true love. He'd had his chance at a lifetime of happiness and blown it.

Unable to bear focusing on the bridal couple or the words of hope and binding ties the priest spoke of, Mac let his gaze wander over the people seated in the several rows in front of the pew he and his immediate family occupied. Thankfully Stephanie Thorton-Stuart was not among those in attendance.

He had sought her out the moment he'd returned to New York to tell her in no uncertain terms that they were not going to happen, and she had seemed to finally accept it. But he wouldn't be surprised if she showed up at Cory's wedding. Though she *had* stopped making statements to the press right after he'd left for Oregon, and they had lost interest. Maybe his mom was right and Stephanie had indeed found a more willing cash-fat fish to fry in her ready-to-go wedding dress. Mac didn't particularly care.

To keep his mind from the woman he *did* care about, he scanned the rest of the guests. Most were related to him in some way, since his father had been one of four brothers, all very reproductively productive. And all of the brothers were still married to their one and only loves, as their father had been before them, as the generations before had. Wasn't that proof of the legend handed down that a MacDougal only loved once?

And even though he turned out to be an aberration in the family, actually capable of loving two women in his lifetime, that feat didn't matter. He'd made an oath to Kate, and he was sticking to it, regardless the cost to him. Kate deserved it for dying too young, when he could have prevented it.

This past week, surrounded by the MacDougal Clan's rough and tumble love as the house filled with relatives showing up for Cory's wedding, Mac had realized exactly how high the price was for keeping his vow. The yearning for a family of his own was nearly too much to bear, and his longing for Ashley, to make that family with her, had increased with each passing day.

If he wanted to keep his sanity, he had no choice but to take off. Even though his leaving again would distress his mom and annoy his business partners. He needed to find some wild, distant place again, a place where he could live the life Kate had been denied.

A place that looked nothing like Oregon. Because with every lush, evergreen forest, with every silently flowing river and every gully he might tumble with his bike down, he'd think of Ashley.

He could do nothing about the loneliness that had burrowed into his soul like a tick since he'd left her.

He shifted again, accidentally elbowing his youngest brother, Brendan. Mac received a sharp elbow to the ribs in return. Brendan's decidedly ornery and normally infectious, challenging grin made Mac's stomach ache. With Ashley's opinion about the importance of family echoing in his head all week, he'd found himself seeing his family in a different way.

He realized just how empty and unfulfilling his form of living life to the maximum had been. His family was an important part of his life, whether he spent much time with them or not, and he would miss them a lot after he left again. He'd miss the laughter, the camaraderie, the caring.

Almost as much as he missed Ashley. What he wouldn't give to hear her laughter, breathe in her scent, and hold her in his arms again.

Damn it.

He had to get control of himself or he'd friggin' bleed to death on the inside.

A loud slam at the back of the church drew everyone's attention.

The huge, carved inner doors had been banged open by a tall, slender woman with wind-tossed blond hair. Carrying what looked like a black overnight bag and wearing a black leather blazer, white shirt, faded blue jeans and black boots, she stood poised at the end of the long aisle. But instead of looking for a place to sit, she was staring hard at the wedding party, who had returned their attentions to the priest. As if her hand suddenly went limp, she dropped the overnight bag to the floor with a thud that echoed among the high rafters of the church.

Thinking his mind was playing tricks on him, Mac turned more fully on the pew and squinted at the woman. She continued to look very much like Ashley

Rivers. *His* Ashley Rivers. But the way her chest rose and fell and her mouth hung open in obvious distress made him doubt his own eyes.

Ashley wouldn't have come all the way to New York and banged her way into a church, and even if she had, she would have never entered it like a bat out of hell or dressed in casual clothing.

The woman lurched forward down the center of the aisle, her wide gaze glued to the bride and groom, drawing the attention once again of those seated toward the back of the large church. A murmur of whispering voices trailed after her.

As she drew nearer, Mac could clearly make out her face. His pulse leapt. Good Lord, it *was* Ashley! But why in the hell was she here and looking so...so *unlike* herself, so crazed?

She raised a hand, and her mouth moved. He wasn't sure, but he thought he heard her say, "Excuse me." She ventured forward a step or two, and a little louder said, "Wait." Then she shocked the hell out of him by rushing forward yelling, "Stop! Please, stop! Mac, you can't marry—this is not—*I object!* Mac!"

His heart in his throat, Mac jumped to his feet and stepped past his gaping mother into the aisle several rows between Ashley and the stunned group at the altar. He held out a reassuring hand to her. "Ashley, I'm here."

Her blue-green eyes went nearly as wide as the *O* she made with her mouth. She jerked her frantic gaze between him and Cory, who was facing her with a scowl on his face while his best man, Mac's other brother, Rory, chuckled.

She pointed a weak finger at his cousin. "But I thought..."

Mac's blood thundered in his ears with the realization that she'd believed he was the one getting married. He waved her toward him. "It's all right, sunshine. MacDougals tend to look alike in our kilts."

His comment broke the tension and had the other guests laughing and nodding knowingly.

Her face flaming as red as he'd ever seen it, she ducked her chin and hurried toward him, undoubtedly because he was closer than any door out. When she reached him she grabbed for his hand with both of hers and squeezed hard, hunkering against him as he guided her into the space his obviously curious family had made on the pew.

She whispered, "Oh my God, Mac. I have never been more embarrassed in my entire life."

He bent toward her ear, momentarily distracted by her wonderful scent. "It's all right." Before he straightened away, he took the time to fill his lungs and his heart with her delicate, flowery scent. He'd thought he would never be this close to her again.

His free hand started to shake, so he covered hers as she continued to clutch his other one. His heart pounded as what she'd done sunk in. She'd come after him. She'd actually come after him. And she'd very impolitely disrupted what she'd thought to be his wedding.

Holy haggis.

His mother leaned toward Ashley, her brown eyes merry, and whispered, "You wouldn't by any chance be Ashley Rivers?"

Mac's mind shouted, *No you're not. Ashley Rivers would have never disrupted a wedding. But Ash Bash sure as hell would have.*

Brendan nearly fell off the pew leaning around their mom to hear Ashley's answer, and Mac's sisters Aileen and Gwen bobbed and dipped trying to see and hear what was going on at his end of the pew. His dad merely grinned at him over their heads.

Her color still high, Ashley gave his mother a weak and ragingly self-conscious smile. "Yes, I am. And I'm so sorry—"

His mother shushed her, reaching around him to pat Ashley on the arm. "Don't be. MacDougals never mind a little excitement." She winked at him. "Especially the good kind."

Mac sent his mom a hard look. He didn't need her adding her matchmaking efforts to the mix. It was going to be hard enough to find a way to send Ashley back home without adding to his sins against her.

Or revealing his feelings.

Feelings he didn't have a right to and couldn't act on anyway.

His mom gave him a blithe smile, then leaned past him again to add, "We'll talk at the reception. If this one—" she poked Mac in the ribs "—doesn't want to go, you can ride with us."

His brother, dad, and sisters nodded in agreement.

With a jerk of his head toward the wedding party to remind his family what they were here for, Mac settled back to watch the rest of the ceremony. Though his mind and every cell in his body remained focused on the glorious woman with her hands entwined with his.

She'd come after him.

The thought kept repeating itself, stirring unwelcome emotions like joy and wonder, emotions he had no business feeling. Suddenly he felt sick to his stomach. Things had become complicated.

It was one thing to walk out of Ashley's life. How in the hell was he going to kick her out of his?

ASHLEY SHOULD HAVE BEEN ill with embarrassment. But as the moments passed and the heat from Mac's hands seeped into hers, all she felt was giddy with the kind of happiness she'd only experienced with him. In that instant, all her doubts fled.

She'd done the right thing, coming to New York. Being with Mac was where she wanted to be for the rest of her life, and she would do anything to convince him that was exactly where she belonged.

Heck, she'd just proved it by barging in on a wedding. Something she would have never done if Mac hadn't given her the courage to be herself.

She leaned toward Mac to better see the groom standing hand in hand with his bride at the altar. With his similar tall, broad-shouldered build, dark-brown hair, and rugged good looks, it was little wonder she'd mistaken him for Mac from a distance. The kilts the groom and most of the groomsmen were wearing had thrown her, too.

She remembered vividly the lilting turn of phrase Mac had used that made her think of a Scotsman. Being a MacDougal, and all, it now made sense. So she couldn't blame herself for thinking it was Mac standing at the altar in his clan's traditional attire.

But when Mac had stood up and stepped into the aisle ahead of her, looking exactly like a Highland lord straight from a lonely girl's fantasies, she couldn't believe she'd made such a mistake. No man on earth could look as wildly beautiful as Wilder Huntington MacDougal V. Her Mac.

She tilted her chin up toward his ear to ask him who the groom was, studiously ignoring his seductively spicy scent and his body's magnetic pull on hers. The heat from the thickly muscled and perfectly hairy bare knee pressed against hers was harder to ignore, and her voice came out breathy when she whispered, "Who is that, anyway?"

He dipped his shoulder and turned his face toward hers, bringing them a hairsbreadth away from cheek to cheek. Memories of his body joined with hers washed over Ashley like a hot summer breeze and she had to fight the urge to nuzzle against him. She had been so right to come after him.

"My cousin, Cory MacDougal, and his soon-to-be wife Deborah Kincaid."

Kincaid. A good Scottish name. Having noted Mac's beautiful mother's dark-red hair, fair skin, and thinking of her comment about Mac's first love not being Scottish—much to his father's distress—a new fear threatened Ashley. She had to know if she faced yet another hurdle.

She couched the question she had to ask in a softly spoken joke. "Are MacDougals only allowed to marry other Scots?"

He straightened to face forward again and shrugged. "Mostly."

Ashley slumped back against the pew, her newfound giddiness dimmed considerably. But she wasn't about to let her lack of proper heritage stand in their way, and considering his family's belief in loving only once, her genealogy was the least of her problems.

She remained silent for the rest of the ceremony, trying not to cry over the words spoken by the bride and groom as they pledged themselves to each other for the rest of their lives. How she wanted to make that vow with Mac. Her heart burned with the need to spend her life with him. She had to convince him to take a chance on her.

She gained solace and hope in the way Mac stroked the back of her hand with his thumb. It seemed such a natural, unconscious motion, she wondered if he even realized he was doing it. Just as she wondered if he realized how much magic danced between them.

When the groom kissed the bride, Mac's thumb stilled and his grip tightened. Yes, he realized what was between them, but he was fighting it.

Because of Kate Wilson.

While Ashley didn't want to diminish what he'd felt for his college sweetheart, she had to encourage him to see that living in the past wasn't healthy. That it was okay to move on. She simply had to get him to admit they were meant to be together. Which wouldn't be simple at all. He carried his stubbornness in the set of his strong jaw, his loyalty in the stiffness of his broad shoulders.

As the newlyweds were joyfully introduced and

everyone rose to applaud the couple's progression down the aisle, Ashley went up on tiptoe to whisper in Mac's ear again. "I need to talk to you."

"And I need to talk to *you*," he returned, his eyes glinting like amber.

The hardness in his gaze sent a dart of fear through her, but she refused to be deterred. She *would* convince him to give them a chance.

As the guests started to file out into the aisle and Mac's stunning family, who really were as gorgeous as he was, peppered her with questions, Mac took hold of her upper arm and pulled her into the aisle. He headed toward the altar instead of the back of the church where everyone else was going.

Her stomach fluttered. If it hadn't been for the flinty look he'd just given her, Ashley might have allowed herself to entertain the fantasy that he was taking her up to the altar to ask her forgiveness, maybe to propose. But she knew in her heart his intent wasn't the stuff of fantasies. He still needed to be reasoned with.

At the altar, he turned right and led her into an antechamber where she guessed the groom and his attendants had readied themselves before the ceremony. Garment bags were either hung from or draped over several of the half dozen dark wooden chairs scattered about, and leather and nylon gym bags lay here and there on the floor.

Ashley gasped. "My overnight bag. I dropped it in the middle of the aisle."

Mac let go of her and closed the heavy, carved door behind them. "Someone will tuck it off to the side.

It'll be fine," he clipped out, his deep voice rich and commanding in the stone antechamber.

Even if she ended up getting right back on a plane to go home, she didn't want to risk losing her things. "It will just take me a second to go grab it." She took a step toward the door.

Mac barred her way. Planting his hands on his hips and frowning at her like a Scottish immortal, he demanded, "What are you doing here, Ashley?"

His displeasure sent the wise, logical, and irrefutable words she'd rehearsed over and over again on the way here up in smoke. She wrapped her arms around her middle to contain the riot of nerves in her stomach. It didn't work. Scrambling to hold onto her courage, she tore her gaze from his hard eyes and focused on the man as a whole.

He was so glorious in his traditional garb. Glorious and intimidating. But she'd been held with tenderness and care for hours by the man she believed in her bones to be the real Wilder MacDougal. She wasn't about to let this crabby giant bluster and scare her into giving up on them.

She pronounced, "I've come to talk to you. And it's important."

"I gathered that when you tried to stop what you thought to be my wedding. Speaking of which, why in the hell did you think that was me?"

She shrugged and tried to ignore the heat seeping into her cheeks. "Your cousin looks like you from far away. Though his calves aren't nearly as bulgy as yours." She smiled, belying the tingling residual of the terror she'd felt when her sleep deprived and anxious mind had latched onto the idea that Mac was the groom at the altar.

"He and my brother Rory prefer race cars over mountain bikes," he explained offhandedly, not responding to her attempt at levity in the least. He gazed intently at her. "Now why did you think I'd be getting married?"

Mortified by her foolishness, the heat in her cheeks intensified. "I thought that maybe you'd decided to listen to what your parents said about you and Stephanie being a good match, and you needing to settle down and get on with your life."

His dark brows slammed together. "How do you know all that?"

"Your mother told me."

He dropped his hands from his hips and his frown deepened. *"My mother?"*

She had never seen him look so fierce. Or so in need of her love. "Yes. Last Sunday. Before I brought you the phone." She hesitated, about to say his mother had also told her about the woman he'd loved, but he started talking before she had a chance.

"Ah, yes, before you brought me the phone, but *after* you told her where I was." He crossed his arms over his chest, his eyes as hard as burnished gold. "I'd begun to believe you were too mature to indulge in payback. Or is that one of your Three P's?"

Annoyance flared at his petty swipe. "No, it's not. But it certainly was the *principled* thing to do." She pulled in a deep breath. She hadn't come all this way to bicker with him. She needed to find a way to bridge the gap between them. "I wasn't trying to get back at you, Mac. I simply needed some answers, and you weren't willing to open up and give them to me. I needed to understand why you were doing what you were doing to me—to us. So I could find a way to deal with it."

"And your way of dealing with it involved forcing me to do my duty to my family."

"No. Not duty. I wanted you to heal your relationship with your family. It had nothing to do with duty." She lowered her own brows and cocked her head at him. "Where did you come up with that?"

"By watching how you live your life, Ashley. By watching you put your duty to your family above everything. Including yourself."

He uncrossed his arms to gesture sharply with his hands. "You'd forced yourself into this cookie cutter shape of what you thought you had to be, not allowing yourself anything that wasn't written in your day planner." He pointed at her, then frowned, obviously noticing that her hands were empty, and the purse she wore strung across her body was far too small to hold even her planner's note pad. "It's in your overnight bag, isn't it? That's why you wanted to go get your bag just now."

Shaking her head, she said softly, "No. It's not." She held her hands out, palms up. "I didn't bring the day planner, Mac. I left it at home."

His dark brows went up and his wonderful mouth quirked. "You're joking."

"No. I don't need it anymore." A surge of confidence and a strange sort of power flooded her, proving the truth of her words. She hadn't once absently reached for the planner or wished she had it.

His skeptical look brought on a wave of frustration that he didn't believe her, that he hadn't seen the risk she'd taken by coming all this way.

She took a step toward him and spread her arms so he'd have to see her, really see her. "I stepped out of my role for you, Mac. I'm here now because I realized I needed to be with you more than I—" her voice cracked "—more than I needed to be there for my family."

She dropped her hands to her sides as a third wave, this time of despair, tried to shove its way through the cracks forming in her resolve. "Even though you never promised me more than a good time."

He groaned and looked up at the ceiling. "That's all I'm able to give you, Ash."

Unwilling to believe it because of what he'd already given her, she skeptically asked, "Why? Because of Kate?"

He glanced back at her sharply, the pain and suspicion raw on his handsome face.

Her heart bled for him, for the burden of mourning he'd weighted himself with. Gently she said, "Your mother also told me about Kate."

He froze, holding himself with an ominous stillness that made her heart pound.

He demanded softly, "What did she tell you?"

She forced the words that were so hard for her to say past her tight throat. "That you loved her. That because you blame yourself for her death you won't get on with your life."

He shook his head, his long, sun-streaked bangs falling across his brow. "It's so much more than that, Ashley."

More? Fear squeezed her throat the rest of the way shut as she felt her chances with him slipping away. The specter of Roger, of his not really wanting her, ratcheted her fear to desperation. "What? Is it me? Am I not the right woman for you to get on with your life with?"

"Oh, Ash, don't. I'm so proud of you for the changes you've made. For ditching that damn planner. You really are incredible." His chest deflated, his resignation palpable. "It has nothing to do with you. It's between me and Kate."

"But Kate is gone, Mac," she whispered, not wanting to dismiss the depth of his feelings. Carefully she moved closer to him, as she imagined one would have to approach a great, injured beast. Because he *was* injured. So terribly, terribly injured.

Ashley needed to heal him more than she needed to breathe. "You know, if you gave it a chance, a MacDougal might actually be able to love twice."

He dropped his gaze, his face a mask of defeat. "I already know that, Ash. A MacDougal *can* love twice."

Her heart exploded in her chest and tears of joy blurred her vision, but she had to be sure. "What are you saying?"

"You know exactly what I'm saying. You got to me, Ash. You got to me good."

Blinking away her tears, Ashley lurched toward him with arms outstretched.

He raised a hand to stop her. "It still won't work. I can't be with you."

She jerked to a halt, confusion and fear warring with her love. She whispered, "Why? As punishment for thinking yourself responsible for Kate's death?"

He scoffed and started to pace the room, his kilt flipping at his knees. "I don't *think* I'm responsible, I *know* I am. If I had agreed to go rock climbing with her for the weekend instead of staying at school to study, she wouldn't have been driving. Which means she wouldn't have fallen asleep at the wheel and she wouldn't have wrapped her car around that damn tree." He looked at her, his eyes swimming in his guilt. "She wouldn't be dead, Ash."

A spurt of self-pity darkened Ashley's heart. If Kate had lived, Ashley would have never known him, would have never found her own heaven in his arms. The thought shamed her. She dropped her chin to her chest and her gaze to the timeworn floor. "And you two would be happily married with a bunch of kids by now."

He made a rude noise and halted his pacing. "I don't know. Kate hadn't been big on settling down."

Understanding dawning, she stated, "But you were."

"Yeah. I was. All my life I'd wanted a big family of my own, just like the one I'd grown up in." He shrugged faintly. "I'd figured I would be able to wear her down."

Ashley pulled in a breath that shored up her resolve. "Mac, you've got to face that she's gone now. You shouldn't continue to deny yourself what you've always wanted. Which happen to be the same things that I want."

He met her gaze, his eyes intense, his mouth unyielding. "I have no choice, Ash. When Kate lay dying in the hospital, her insides so scrambled there was nothing they could do for her, she asked me to make her a promise. And I did. I made a vow to her right before she died. With her hand in mine."

Ashley's terror returned, stiffening her muscles as sure as death. "What was the vow?"

"That I would live the life she'd been robbed of, live it to the max. That I would live for her, Ash. So you see, even if I wanted to, I can't make a life with you, or anyone else for that matter. I've sworn to live for Kate."

Her heart shattering into a million pieces, all Ashley could think was a MacDougal might love twice, but she would forever come second.

Chapter Fourteen

Fear, frustration, confusion and hurt rolled across Ashley's beautiful face with the force of a ravaging storm. Mac fisted his hands against the urge to reach for her.

He hated this. He hated having to say these things to her, adding further insult to the injury he'd done to her. Hated watching her harden before his very eyes as she fought to keep her composure. But she had to understand. He had to make her accept there was no hope for them, despite what they both might want.

He put all his regret into his expression and voice. "I'm sorry, Ash. I wish it could be different."

Her tear-filled eyes narrowed, piercing him with her distrust. "Do you, Mac? Do you really?"

Unable to bear the cold cynicism in her voice, he took the steps to close the gap between them and gripped her upper arms, the black leather of her coat soft but cold beneath his palms. "Yes, damn it." His voice cracked. "More than I want my next breath."

Her shimmering gaze intensified, boring into his. "Then make it different."

His gut twisted, but he forced himself to keep meeting her harsh gaze. "I can't, Ash. You know I can't."

She shrugged out of his grasp and stepped away, her finely made chin high. "No, I don't know. Just like I don't know how any woman who'd claimed to love you could have asked such a thing of you." She lowered her chin and shook her head in obvious puzzlement. "I can't believe she would want anything for you but happiness."

Before he could defend Kate's wants the door to the antechamber inched open. Rory stuck his head through the crack, his eyes darting warily between the room's occupants as if he expected vases and statues of saints to be flying.

Closest to Mac in age, with not quite two years separating them, Rory was the most likely to be able to read Mac on the spot. Next to Ashley being able to tell what drove him, that was the last thing Mac needed at the moment. Mac barked at him. "Go away, Rory."

His brother came the rest of the way into the room, instead. Raising a hand, he said, "I just need my stuff, Mac. Then you two can get back to—" his light brown gaze darted between Mac and Ashley, whose attempt at a pleasant, *why-no-I'm-not-upset* smile was growing twitchy around the edges "—to whatever it is you're doing." Since he'd just lost his partner in moral crime to wedded bliss, Rory was probably anxious to get changed and go off and drown his sorrows.

Mac blew out a breath and waved Rory in, but when Brendan followed on his heels and their mother appeared in the doorway, next, Mac knew it was mostly a reconnaissance mission. He stomped toward the nearest gym bag and scooped it up, tossing it to Brendan to get his blatantly curious gaze off Ashley.

A surge of possessiveness coursed through Mac and added to his frustration. He wanted Ashley to move on with her life, but not with his randy and women-spoiled brothers, and he sure as hell didn't want to know about it.

With him shoving bags and jackets at them, Mac had them heading back out the door before they had the chance to ask any of the questions he could see clear as day in their faces. He didn't dare look at his mother long enough to gauge what was on her mind before he closed the heavy door again.

Ashley noisily let out the breath she'd obviously been holding and paced away, her long legs endless in her jeans and her black boots sounding hard against the stone-tiled floor. She measured the length of the room, then paused, growing still. She looked at him speculatively, her arched brows drawn together. "Did it ever occur to you that you might have misinterpreted what she was asking of you?" She jumped right back into the argument like only a woman can.

His insides withered at the memory of those last moments, of the brief minute of clarity in Kate's drug-hazed gaze, of the limpness of her hand as she slipped away. The pain, the impotent rage, the guilt were never far away. "How could I have misinterpreted *live for me, Mac?* Her last words are etched on my soul, Ash. I seriously doubt I got them wrong."

Ashley tilted her head back and closed her eyes. "Oh, my—" She broke off with a half laugh, half sob. "You didn't get her words wrong, Mac. It was catching her meaning that you blew." She lowered her chin and met his gaze, understanding shining in her dark-aqua eyes. "I'd bet my family's health that any woman worthy—" her voice hitched and his heart gave an answering jerk "—of your love would never ask you to sacrifice your future like that."

She moved back in front of him and took his hands in hers. Her slender fingers were icy cold despite the flush in her cheeks. "Mac, have you ever considered that Kate was asking you to *live* for her, not live *for her?*"

Mac froze, her words blazing a hot trail through his brain. The notion slammed into him like the sidewalk on a base jump gone wrong. He shook his head and tried to back away, but she wouldn't release her hold on his hands.

Her gaze bored into his. "Are you sure you didn't latch on to your interpretation of what she'd said because you didn't want to let go?"

"Of course I don't want to let go. I didn't want her to die."

"Oh, Mac. I know." She squeezed his hands, her strength surprising and compelling. "But she did. It was her time. There is nothing any of us can do about that." She pulled in a shuddering breath. "And now it's time for you to let her go."

The pain and guilt that had had a starring role in his life drama screamed foul. He closed his eyes against her opposing hope. He couldn't do as she asked.

She eased her grip and started caressing his palm with her thumb. "I know it's hard."

Her touch started a yearning that spread from his hands to every inch of his body. He fought the longing, knowing it wouldn't do either one of them any good; hanging on to a sheer cliff with his fingertips had been easier.

Her voice was soft and soothing. "It was hard for me to let go of my mom, to accept that she's in a better place. But I know she would want me to."

He opened his eyes to the understanding glowing in her blue-green gaze. His knees threatened to buckle. It took all his strength to lock them and stand tall against her caring.

"Kate would have surely wanted you to move on and find happiness." She tilted her head, her silky blond hair curving on one shoulder like soft gold. "If the roles had been reversed, you would have wanted her to be happy, wouldn't you?"

Her words tempted him to sway to her way of thinking. She tugged on his hands to draw him near again, but he couldn't budge, physically or emotionally. He didn't dare. He couldn't betray Kate so easily.

The spirit of the woman he'd worked so hard to free from her prison of refinement and control blazed in Ashley's eyes, and she stepped toward him, eliminating the space he'd put between them. "It's time to stop running away from life, Mac. It's time to take a chance again."

The very thought of taking such a chance left him struggling for his next breath like a man caught in a raging river. He mentally piled on the sandbags to shore up his defenses against her flood of logic. "I'm not about to just forget my promise." He shook his head. "I can't."

"You don't have to forget about anything, especially not Kate. I would never ask that of you. That would be so wrong. She's part of who you are now, the wild man I fell in love with."

Her declaration knocked the air from his lungs and set his heart pounding. She loved him? Dear God, he couldn't deny the soul-melting joy her words brought him, but he still couldn't let them matter.

She yanked on his hands to regain his attention. "But you need to stop living in the past and start looking toward the future. I want to be in that future, Mac. I want to be with you."

A future spent with Ashley would be heaven on earth. He didn't deserve that kind of reward. He blinked hard to clear his mind of the fog of possibilities. He had to make her see reason, to acknowledge the truth of what he'd put her through. "For God's sake, why would you want to be with me? I've done nothing but lie to you and hurt you."

"Were the things that you said to me out on the basketball court lies? The things about me deserving more in life than what I'd laid out for myself?"

He shook his head with the strength of his conviction. "No. I meant every word. You deserve a hell of a lot more than you were allowing—"

He halted when he noticed a sweet smile of victory playing at the corners of her full mouth. "Kind of like what you deserve, right?"

He looked away as he slipped into the crevasse of wanting Ashley created inside of him, falling deeper into the place he shouldn't allow himself to go. The soft touch of her hand on his cheek made him look at her again. She was so beautiful. So beautiful and understanding and caring and everything else he'd ever wanted.

He couldn't have her. He tried to swallow the bitter lump of guilt swelling in his throat, but it wouldn't go down. "No, I don't deserve happiness. I let Kate down."

She clenched her eyes shut, then whirled and paced away from him. "You didn't let her down! Accidents happen, Mac. Bad things happen to very, very good people." She cut the air with her hand. "You can't just throw your life away, too."

The image of Ashley standing behind her father's desk, dutifully filling in his calendar, came to mind. "Look who's talking."

She stormed back toward him. "That's right." She aimed a finger at the center of her own chest. "Look who's talking. I admit now that I denied who I was to gain my father's approval. That I took the safe way out by stepping into my mother's shoes and giving up on a future of my own after that jerk, Roger's betrayal.

"But because of you—" she flattened her hand over her heart "—because of the things you make me feel and want, I took a chance and stepped back into *my* life. I faced my fears head-on, and even though they won when you—" she faltered, but after a few quick breaths continued "—you admitted your lies and left, I didn't give up. I didn't run and hide again."

She stepped closer and leveled her finger at him. "You're not living the way you are because it's what you think Kate wanted. You're using that vow as a shield." She poked him once, then dropped her hand. "Just like I used my planner."

Her accusation and admission sent his mind reeling, but she didn't give him time to latch on to any one thing.

"You keep saying you failed her." She fisted her hands and planted them on her hips. "Well, I think you hold yourself away from those who love you because you're afraid. You're afraid to risk failing someone again. That vow doesn't prove your worth any more than my day planner proved mine."

Stunned by her words, Mac could only stare at her with a locked jaw.

Her fisted hands slipped from her hips as despair joined the anger in her eyes. "You know what, Mac? You're never going to truly fulfill your vow to Kate if you don't get over your fear. And neither one of us will get what we deserve out of life."

She turned and headed for the door. Without looking at him, she said, "You can stick that on your bike and ride it, Mr. MacDougal."

In all her Ash-Bash glory, she yanked the heavy, carved door open, stepped through the doorway and pulled the door shut with a slam behind her. The sound reverberated in his head and his heart.

She was gone. Maybe forever.

Mac buried both hands in his hair, wanting to deny what Ashley had said. But her words bombarded him, forcing him to consider them.

Had he misunderstood what Kate had been asking of him? Had she wanted him to *live* for her, not live *for her?* He scrubbed his face with his hands. Jeez, talk about semantics.

Kate had been so full of life, so focused on living life to the maximum, would she have really wanted him to give up the possibility of loving again, of having a family?

No, she wouldn't.

Feeling broad-sided and weak-kneed, Mac plopped down in the nearest chair, knocking his brother's missed brown leather bomber jacket from the chair's high back onto the floor. So he had misinterpreted Kate's final request for ten years. Why? Was he afraid to fail?

Hell, no. There wasn't a mountain he wouldn't take a shot at conquering or a corporation he wouldn't storm on Wall Street.

Or a woman he wouldn't go after if he really wanted her.

Oh, man. He'd been an absolute idiot.

His gaze flew to the door. Ashley was gone. His heart lurched, sending blood thundering through his body. A cold dread gripped his gut. Mac was forced to admit, once and for all, that he wasn't afraid to fail someone, he was afraid to lose that someone again.

The chair clattered on uneven legs when he shoved to his feet and bolted for the door. He couldn't let her leave. He couldn't lose her.

He headed into the sanctuary, his gaze darting everywhere. Aside from the church's cleanup crew removing Cory's wedding decorations to prepare for the next ceremony, the sanctuary was empty. Panic dimmed his vision. God help him, she couldn't be gone already.

He ran down the aisle with his kilt flapping up at his knees, terrified that if he didn't catch up with her now, he might never get her back.

GRIPPING THE EDGE of the tall, slender table in the church vestibule with her free hand, Ashley signed her name after the short apology she'd written in the guest book as neatly as she could with shaking hands. She prayed her quick explanation that she'd mistaken Cory MacDougal for his cousin, Wilder, would somewhat make up for her disrupting what should have been a perfect moment for the bride and groom.

A moment Ashley had serious doubts about experiencing herself. Her throat closed and her vision blurred. If she couldn't convince Mac to give them a chance, she really would end up living her life through her family, because she knew in her soul that she would never stop loving him.

She would never be happy with anyone except her wild man.

The knowledge restored her determination, but she wasn't sure what to do next. She returned the pen to its holder and considered her options. She could hail a taxi to take her to a hotel, or she could go outside and accept Mary MacDougal's invitation to attend the wedding reception with them, assuming the MacDougals were amongst the crowd she could hear milling on the steps in front of the church. Perhaps getting acquainted with Mac's family would help her further her case with him.

One thing she didn't want to do next, though, was see Mac. The fight had all gone out of her for now. And Mac needed time to think about what she'd said. Maybe he would come to his senses on his own if she gave him some space.

Maybe not.

Her heart quelled at the possibility. Forcibly shaking off the negativity, she decided that she should find out where the reception was being held. Then she could swing past a clothing boutique and buy something more appropriate to wear before she crashed the reception. She'd caused enough stir for the day.

She picked up her overnight bag that had indeed been set off to the side for her, turned from the guest book table, and jumped when the doors to the sanctuary burst open next to her. Mac charged into the outer room, his focus on the next set of huge doors leading outside, drawing her startled gaze. The noise of the inner doors banging open wasn't nearly as startling to her as the pure panic etched on his face.

His obvious distress made her heart pound. She called out to him. "Mac!"

He whirled toward her and the tightness in his jaw and fear in his eyes immediately eased. He closed the distance between them in all of two steps and reached for her. He wrapped his arms around her, lifting her from her feet in a crushing embrace. "You didn't leave," he breathed into her hair.

Fighting for air, more because of a heart gone mad than the strength of his arms, she forced out, "No, not yet."

He squeezed tighter. "Don't. Don't leave, Ash. Ever."

Tears of joy blinded her and she prayed she already knew what he meant. But she needed to hear the words, needed to be absolutely sure she understood his intentions. Her heart couldn't take another crushing blow. "What are you saying, Mac?" she croaked, crazy hope rioting through her.

He loosened his hold enough to let her slip down his front until her feet were back on the floor and she could look up at him. She met his gaze and gasped. The fear and hope and love she saw in his eyes sent hot tears slipping down her cheeks.

He pulled one arm from around her and reached up to gently wipe a tear away with the rough pad of his thumb. So tender. So loving. So Mac.

He cupped her cheek with his hand. "I'm saying I want you to stay. In my life. Forever."

She nuzzled against the warmth of his palm, her heart soaring with the birds amongst the church bells.

"You were right, Ash. I *was* afraid, but not of failing. I was afraid of losing again." He let out a harsh laugh, then dropped his forehead against hers. "If I let you walk out of my life…I can't imagine a worse loss. You've filled up the holes in my heart so much it feels like it's about to burst." His voice deepened to a rough scrape and he lifted his other hand to hold her face. "Say you forgive me?"

Before she could force an answer past the love clogging her throat, he barreled on. "I'm so sorry for the lies—"

She cut him off. "It's okay, Mac—"

"No, it's not okay. I'll never lie to you again. For any reason. I love you, Ashley. And I know now that I'll be able to put the past to rest—as long as you'll spend the future with me. As my wife. I want to marry you, Ash-Bash. I want to spend my life with you." He raised his forehead from hers and kissed her sweetly on the lips. "The woman who'd been able to love the dirty guy on a bike."

The last barrier to their life together roared up in her mind. Her voiced quavered as she admitted, "But I'm not Scottish."

His grin was wicked and wonderful. "No. But our children will be. At least by half."

Happiness bubbled out of her on a laugh. "Oh, Mac—"

He kissed her again, this time hard and deep and totally inappropriate for an unmarried couple standing within the walls of a church.

She pulled away, gasping for breath and her cheeks blazing hot. But when she met the warm glow of his incredible topaz eyes, she couldn't resist the wildness spreading through her from the power of her love for him.

"Yes, I'll marry you, Wilder Huntington Mac-Dougal V." She reached a hand down and tugged at the elaborately decorated leather pouch she was pretty sure was called a sporran. "But only if you wear a kilt."

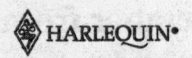

HARLEQUIN
AMERICAN *Romance*

presents a brand-new series by
Cathy Gillen Thacker

The Deveraux Legacy

Steeped in Southern tradition, the Deveraux family legacy is generations old and about to be put to the test.

Don't miss:

HER BACHELOR CHALLENGE
September 2002

HIS MARRIAGE BONUS
October 2002

MY SECRET WIFE
November 2002

THEIR INSTANT BABY
December 2002

And look for a special Harlequin single title in April 2003.

Available wherever
Harlequin books are sold.

HARLEQUIN®
Makes any time special®

Visit us at www.eHarlequin.com

HARTDL

Continuing in September from

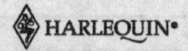

HARLEQUIN

AMERICAN *Romance*

WELCOME to Harmony

the heartwarming series by
Sharon Swan

Come back to Harmony, Arizona, a little town with lots of surprises!

Abby Prentiss is about to walk down the aisle with the perfect man...until her ex-husband shows up on the doorstep of her bed-and-breakfast. But Ryan Larabee doesn't know he was once married to Abby—because Ryan has amnesia! What's a bride-to-be to do? Find out in...

HUSBANDS, HUSBANDS...EVERYWHERE!

Available September 2002 wherever Harlequin books are sold.

HARLEQUIN®
Makes any time special®

Visit us at www.eHarlequin.com

HARHHE

Beginning in September from

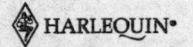

HARLEQUIN®

AMERICAN *Romance*®

Serving their country,
as they follow their hearts...

GROOMS IN UNIFORM

a new series of romantic adventure by
Mollie Molay

Enjoy all three titles in this new series:

A duchess crosses swords with the naval officer
assigned to protect her in

THE DUCHESS & HER BODYGUARD
On sale September 2002

A special-agent-in-charge surrenders his heart
to a feisty free spirit in

SECRET SERVICE DAD
On sale November 2002

Look for the third title in this delightful series in January 2003.

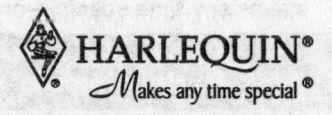

HARLEQUIN®
*M*akes any time special®

Visit us at www.eHarlequin.com

HARGIU

eHARLEQUIN.com

buy books | authors | online reads | community | membership | learn to write

magazine

♥ quizzes
Is he the one? What kind of lover are you? Visit the **Quizzes** area to find out!

♥ recipes for romance
Get scrumptious meal ideas with our **Recipes for Romance**.

♥ romantic movies
Peek at the **Romantic Movies** area to find Top 10 Flicks about First Love, ten Supersexy Movies, and more.

♥ royal romance
Get the latest scoop on your favorite royals in **Royal Romance**.

♥ games
Check out the **Games** pages to find a ton of interactive romantic fun!

♥ romantic travel
In need of a romantic rendezvous? Visit the **Romantic Travel** section for articles and guides.

♥ lovescopes
Are you two compatible? Click your way to the **Lovescopes** area to find out now!

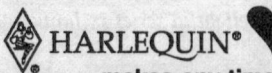

HARLEQUIN®

makes any time special—online...

Visit us online at
www.eHarlequin.com

HINTMAG

Coming in August...

UNBREAKABLE BONDS

by

Judy Christenberry

Identical twin brothers separated at birth. One had every opportunity imaginable. One had nothing, except the ties of blood. Now fate brings them back together as part of the Randall family, where they are thrown into a maelstrom of divided loyalties, unexpected revelations and the knowledge that some bonds are simply unbreakable.

Dive into a new chapter of the bestselling series *Brides for Brothers* with this unforgettable story.

Available August 2002 wherever paperbacks are sold.

HARLEQUIN®
Makes any time special®

Visit us at www.eHarlequin.com

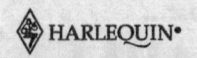

HARLEQUIN
AMERICAN *Romance*

How do you marry a Hardison?

First you tempt him. Then you tame him...
all the way to the altar.

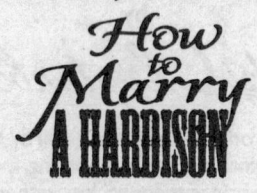

How to Marry A HARDISON

by
Kara Lennox

The handsome Hardison brothers are about to meet their matches when three Texas ladies decide to stop at nothing to lasso one of these most eligible bachelors.

Watch for:

VIXEN IN DISGUISE
August 2002

PLAIN JANE'S PLAN
October 2002

SASSY CINDERELLA
December 2002

Don't miss Kara Lennox's HOW TO MARRY A HARDISON series, available wherever Harlequin books are sold.

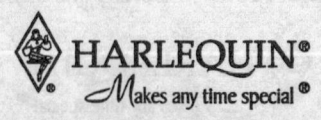

HARLEQUIN®
Makes any time special®

Visit us at www.eHarlequin.com

HARHTMAH